Eddie

The Lost Youth of Edgar Allan Poe

WRITTEN AND ILLUSTRATED BY

 SCOTT GUSTAFSON

SIMON & SCHUSTER
BOOKS FOR YOUNG READERS

NEW YORK   LONDON   TORONTO   SYDNEY

SIMON & SCHUSTER BOOKS FOR YOUNG READERS
An imprint of Simon & Schuster Children's Publishing Division
1230 Avenue of the Americas, New York, New York 10020
This book is a work of fiction. Any references to historical events, real people,
or real locales are used fictitiously. Other names, characters, places, and incidents
are products of the author's imagination, and any resemblance
to actual events or locales or persons, living or dead, is entirely coincidental.
SIMON & SCHUSTER BOOKS FOR YOUNG READERS is a trademark of Simon & Schuster, Inc.
For information about special discounts for bulk purchases, please contact Simon &
Schuster Special Sales at 1-866-506-1949 or business@simonandschuster.com.
The Simon & Schuster Speakers Bureau can bring authors to your live event.
For more information or to book an event, contact the Simon & Schuster Speakers
Bureau at 1-866-248-3049 or visit our website at www.simonspeakers.com.

Book design by Laurent Linn
The text for this book is set in Minister.
The illustrations were rendered on smooth, two-ply bristol board
using graphite pencils and Derivan ® Liquid Pencil.
Manufactured in the United States of America
0711 FFG
2 4 6 8 10 9 7 5 3 1
Library of Congress Cataloging-in-Publication Data
Gustafson, Scott.
Eddie : the lost youth of Edgar Allan Poe / written and illustrated by
Scott Gustafson.—1st ed.
p. cm.
Summary: Edgar Poe, aided by the imp McCobber, has twenty-four hours
to prove himself innocent of an act of mischief committed at the home of the judge
who lives beside John Allan, foster father of the orphaned author-to-be.
ISBN 978-1-4169-9764-1
ISBN 978-1-4169-9766-5 (eBook)
1. Poe, Edgar Allan, 1809–1849—Childhood and youth—Juvenile fiction.
[1. Poe, Edgar Allan, 1809–1849—Childhood and youth—Fiction.
2. Demonology—Fiction. 3. Orphans—Fiction. 4. Authors—Fiction.
5. Mystery and detective stories.] I. Title.
PZ7.G982127Edd 2011   [Fic]—dc22   2010037390

FIRST
EDITION

The Master of the Macabre

THIS IS EDGAR ALLAN POE: scholar, editor, author, poet, and pioneer of American literature. But it isn't for these accomplishments that he is best remembered. Horror stories are what people think of when they hear the name Poe: grisly, terrifying horror stories. His just happen to be some of the scariest ever written. It is because of these tales that Edgar Allan Poe has been dubbed the "Master of the Macabre."

Macabre is a great word. It refers to things that are ghastly, gruesome, and disturbingly frightening. Poe's stories at their best are all that and more.

But why Poe? you might ask. Why after almost two hundred years and thousands of horror stories by other authors does the work of Edgar Allan Poe still tingle our spines and make us squirm?

For that question there is, of course, no simple answer. Writers, like all other people, are very complicated characters. And yet, Poe had something extra, a gift that set him apart from other writers of his day and from those of future generations.

But part of the answer, at least, can be found in one of his own short stories entitled, "The Imp of the Perverse."

If you have ever stood at the window in a tall building, or on the brink of a scenic mountain overlook, you may have heard a small voice whisper, "Go ahead, jump!" Then, most likely, you also felt that chilling jab in the gut as you, just for a moment, imagined yourself plummeting over the edge. If so, dear reader, you too may have had a brush with what Poe called the Imp of the Perverse.

Now, most people know just how to deal with this nasty little demon; they ignore it and it scurries back into the dark corners of the imagination from which it crept.

But that's where Poe was different. When his imp suggested that he jump out of a window, Edgar not only paused to listen, but also engaged the little fiend in a lively conversation. Together they lingered on the edge and peered over. And then they got creative. While Edgar imagined himself hurtling through the air, they each took turns adding grisly details to the fall. Until finally, after crashing through tree limbs and bouncing off boulders, he came to his bone-splintering, imaginary end.

But it didn't stop there. Together, Poe and his imp poked into those dark corners of the imagination then peered, by flickering candlelight, at the gruesome and terrifying things they found there. As the imp rousted the menacing shadows and faceless horrors into the light, Edgar the author got to work, writing detailed descriptions and weird stories of all that swirled and slithered within view of his mind's eye.

And it wasn't just creepy things that got them going. The simplest things fed this duo's dark imagination—costume parties, clammy cellars, a family pet, and

the beating of a human heart—all inspired wonderful tales of murder and mayhem. Such horror classics as "Hop Frog," "The Cask of Amontillado," "The Black Cat," and "The Tell-Tale Heart" all sprang from such seemingly innocent beginnings.

And yet all this still doesn't solve the puzzle that is or was Edgar Allan Poe. To truly unravel that life of mystery and imagination, we have to start at the beginning, when the man was just a boy, and when Edgar was called Eddie. For before Poe became the Master of the Macabre, it seemed that the Macabre was master of him.

Prologue

IT WAS COLD THE NIGHT EDGAR POE WAS BORN. January 9, 1809, was bitter cold in Boston. The child's parents, David and Elizabeth Poe, were actors, and acting meant constant travel. Touring the country, theater by theater, they might play for a night, a week, or a month, but then they always moved on.

Edgar and his older brother, Henry, had been born into that theatrical life, much like their English mother before them. As a girl of nine, Elizabeth had begun her professional stage career. Petite and pretty, she was an audience favorite from the very beginning. David, her husband, on the other hand, was not so lucky. As a young man, he left the study of law for the love of the stage. Unfortunately, the stage, or more precisely the critics, did not love him in return.

And then, there was the drinking. More and more frequently, just before an evening's performance, an announcement had to be made. "The part that was to be played by Mr. David Poe will be played by another actor instead. Unfortunately, Mr. Poe is indisposed this evening."

"Indisposed" was a polite way of saying he was drunk.

Sometime in 1810, David Poe deserted his family. History has no record of where he went or what he did, but at some point before he left, he must have paused to bid his sons good night. Through a haze of alcohol he swayed up the boardinghouse stairs, then on to his sleeping boys' bedside.

As he leaned to kiss each good night, a thing, tiny and quick, flitted from the father to Eddie. As it turned out, David Poe left his youngest son something to remember him by—one of his own demons. And the little demon, otherwise known as the imp . . . why, he was there to stay.

There, in the dark, young Edgar's new companion nestled close.

"Ahh, this is cozy," the imp purred. "By the way, the name's McCobber and ya know, Eddie me lad, I think this is the beginning of a beautiful friendship."

The imp snuggled next to the boy's ear and pulled the covers up to his chin. Eddie soon learned that he and he alone was the only one who could hear or see McCobber.

Life as an actress in early nineteenth-century America was already difficult enough for Elizabeth Poe, and the stress and hard times began taking their toll. Whether her husband had realized it or not, he had also left her expecting a third child. Somehow Elizabeth managed to keep working during her pregnancy and within a week of baby Rosalie's birth, she was back on stage. By the fall of 1811, she was unable to care for all three children and work, so her oldest boy, Henry, had gone to live with his grandparents. Elizabeth, along with Eddie and Rosalie, joined a group of players in Richmond who were planning to tour the south that winter. She started rehearsals, but illness had left her too weak to take the stage.

With every passing day she grew weaker, and on the morning of December 8, Elizabeth Poe made her final farewell. Homes were found for the now-orphaned Poe children. Henry would continue to live with his grandparents in Baltimore, Rosalie went to the Mckenzies in Richmond, while Eddie was taken in by Frances and John Allan of Richmond.

John Allan had, at first, said no to his wife's idea of bringing this three-year-old boy into their otherwise

childless home. But Frances was very persuasive. So, on December 9, these two well-meaning strangers took home a young orphan named Edgar Poe, though John Allan never officially adopted Edgar Poe.

McCobber, on the other hand, welcomed Eddie into his itty-bitty impish heart like a long lost member of the family. The boy was smart, quick-witted, and had an imagination that just wouldn't quit. And Eddie responded. The pair became fast friends.

As Eddie grew, so did the little demon's influence. Everything the boy experienced—home, school, friends—all were seen through the lens of the imp's slanted vision. Eddie's world took on a decidedly McCobber tone. Monsters lurked in every corner. Teachers couldn't appreciate his genius and jealous schoolmates hated him because he was too clever. The night wind moaned for his soul and dead branches waved him closer, waiting only to ensnare him.

And then, upon a midnight dreary, everything changed.

It was a stormy night, and Eddie and McCobber were well into their second nightmare of the evening when suddenly they were awakened. Years later, as an adult, Edgar the poet would write of it as a "gentle rapping," but in reality it was more like a cold, wet *thwack*.

The boy opened his eyes to see the black shape of a dazed bird, flapping helplessly outside his rain-splattered window.

Grabbing a towel from the washstand in his room, Eddie opened the window and enfolded the wet, storm-battered bird into the soft, dry cloth.

All the while McCobber ranted and raved, "Stop! What are you doing?" He fumed. "Get away from that thing. Look at those claws! . . . And that beak—it'll rip your throat out!"

Oddly, for once, Eddie paid no attention to his demon companion. Gently, the boy carried the slowly reviving bird in.

"NO!" screamed McCobber. "Throw it out, I tell ya, before it's too late!"

"Well, forevermore . . . ," said the raven, not quite trusting his refocusing eyes. "What's with that little jerk?"

At that moment, two things became perfectly clear to Eddie. After all these years, somebody else had finally seen the imp. He wasn't imagining it, and he wasn't crazy. And the other thing . . . he had just made a new friend.

The town, the street, and the houses were all dark and quiet, all except one. In the attic window of the Allan house, a candle burned as the young Edgar Poe grappled with a rhyme. His ink-stained fingers clutched a quill that scratched out yet another unsatisfactory verse, while his other hand propped up the head of the struggling poet. The wondrous words that had crowded his brain earlier that night were gone. They seemed to have slipped through his fingers and flown out the open window into the night, or at least, wherever they had gone, they were now beyond his reach.

Just a few short hours before, he had crept up the stairs to this makeshift attic study for a nightly

CHAPTER ONE

rendezvous with his imagination. At that point the words, his words, had come to him so fast and furiously that he had barely had enough time to scribble them down. The rush of creativity had made him feel as if he were flying. He had soared on the wings of inspiration. Every word that had flowed from his pen had felt absolutely perfect, landing with grace and beauty upon the white page.

But now, as he read and reread those same lines, they stiffened, curled up, and died—becoming lifeless black squiggles on the shroud of paper. In disgust he ripped the offending scrawl from the roll of otherwise clean paper, crumpled the piece, and then tossed it into the graveyard of similar wads that lay at his feet.

"Ah, why don't you just quit!" a small, unpleasant voice rasped in the boy's ear. "Call it a night and hit the hay. Or, better yet, let's climb up onto the roof and howl at the moon!"

"Arrgh!" Eddie flopped backward into the dusty upholstery and exhaled a frustrated sigh. "Where did it go? I almost had it. The words were right here. . . . They were so sweet. . . . Now they're not only sour, but they're rotten and they stink!"

"Ah, maybe you're all washed up!" the voice tossed in.

"Shut up, McCobber!" Eddie ran his fingers through his hair and, sighing once more, sank farther back into his chair. "Some help you are."

"Nice way to talk to your old pal," McCobber said, pretending to be hurt. "Why, who is at your shoulder day in and day out, helping you through all the hard times by offering you his many centuries' worth of sage advice?"

"Hmmm . . ." Eddie was not listening. He was watching as the flickering candle flame made the strange shapes of Uncle Galt's collection appear to move and breathe.

His foster father's rich uncle had a passion for collecting. Years ago, long before Eddie had come to live with the Allans, Uncle Galt had started what learned men called a "cabinet of curiosities." He had filled it with fossils, natural specimens, ancient relics, and whatnot. But long ago the collection had outgrown the cabinet, or even a closet, and it was now stored in the back rooms of several buildings that Uncle Galt owned, as well as here in the Allans' attic. John Allan called it a rat's nest, and had it not been for all the favors he owed the old man, he would have gladly chucked every scrap of it into the street.

Eddie, however, loved it. The dusty fossils, the moth-eaten specimens, the musty antiques, and the sooty old paintings all held secrets from past lives. That was one of the reasons Eddie had carved out a little niche for himself up here. He found inspiration nestled in the moldering decay.

Eddie's thoughts drifted as he absentmindedly ran his fingers over the battered face of an old devil puppet that hung from the rafters near his chair. It was part of a set of hand puppets once used by a traveling puppeteer. Eddie had seen a show something like it on a street corner when he was younger.

"I'll bet you were a real star in your day," Eddie thought out loud. He smiled at the gruesomely funny features. "You probably saw more of the world from your puppet stage than most humans ever will. . . . If you could only talk. . . ." He sighed.

"Yeah," McCobber interjected sarcastically. "I bet that *would* be fascinating. Hey, maybe he could tell us what it's like to have sweaty puppeteer fingers wiggling around in your head."

On second thought, Eddie decided, maybe it was best that this devil couldn't speak. Eddie personally had more talking devils than he needed.

McCobber stretched. Looking from Eddie's shoulder into the night, he yawned and said, "Aaahh, it's late, laddie. Maybe that little prince of darkness doesn't need his beauty rest, but I—YONNIE CO-HONNIE, DID YOU SEE THAT? THERE'S A MONSTER OVER THERE!"

Eddie shot forward in his chair and peered out the open window. Across the backyard in the boarding-house next door, all was dark—with the exception of a single light burning in a lone window.

"Where?" he asked. "I don't—"

"THERE!" McCobber shouted. "LOOK! There's a monster in that house, I tell ya!"

Eddie watched in horror as indeed a truly monstrous shadow moved across the drawn window shade.

"I told you!" McCobber yanked on Eddie's ear and waved wildly. "Look at that hairy fiend, will ya! That's no man. It's not even an animal. It's . . . It's some kind of . . . a . . . a . . . a WEREWOLF! Just look at it hulking around over there. By Godfrey, I hope it doesn't come through that window!" The little imp was frantic now and barely able to keep his balance on the boy's shoulder.

"Look, look. . . . What's it doing? It just lunged for something. CRIMONETTELY! It just caught a poor little bird in its clutches . . . and . . . and . . . Ahhh, jeez! Did you see that? That horrid creature just swallowed a wee, helpless bird! It was HORRIBLE. That big shadow just swallowed the little shadow. Oh, ICCK! . . . WAIT! WHERE'D HE GO?" McCobber's horrified eyes bulged from their sockets. "I bet he saw us! Jeez-loweez. I just know it! He's comin' for us!"

The poor imp dove behind Eddie's collar and peeked out. He cried, in a fear-strangled whisper, "Quick, Eddie boy! Douse that light!"

Suddenly there was a rush of air, as a flapping black shape burst from the darkness and landed on the sill next to them.

"AAAAAHHHH!" McCobber screamed in Eddie's ear, the boy started.

"Are you boys still up?" It was Eddie's pet raven, returning from a late-night outing.

"Whew." Eddie exhaled in relief. "Raven, it's just you!" He took another deep breath and hoped his heartbeat would slow to a normal rate.

"What's going on?" Raven asked, smiling. "You lads look like you've just seen a ghost."

"We've just seen an evil bird-eatin' monster, that's all!" spat McCobber.

"Up to your old tricks, eh, Mac?" The raven shook his head. "Listen, Impy, why don't you lay off and let the kid get some sleep? It's a school night, you know."

"Why, you yolk-brained moron!" McCobber growled. "I wish you'd land that fat feathered carcass of yours on the windowsill across the way there. Then we'd see how smart you are. . . . Go on. Once you're a midnight snack, we can all get some peace!"

"What windowsill?" Raven asked, looking across the yard at the dark houses. The window was now dark.

"That one over there, it . . . ," McCobber began.

"Forget it," Eddie said, shaking his head. "It was probably nothing."

He capped his ink bottle, then stretched and yawned.

"Raven is right, McCobber.
It's time for bed."

McCobber started to protest, but the boy
cut him off—"Say good night, McCobber"—as he
picked up the candle.

"Ah, good night," he snarled, "but I hope that
monster finds you where you sleep and drags you
flappin' and screamin' from your snug little nest—"

"And a good night to you, too, McCobber." The raven smiled. "Sleep well, Eddie."

"Good night, Raven." Eddie had crossed the room, had lifted the trapdoor, and was heading down the narrow attic stairway.

"By the way, Satan Junior," Raven called in a loud whisper from the windowsill, "how about you keep a lid on the nightmare action so Eddie can get a little rest tonight."

McCobber started fuming.

"Just say good night, McCobber," Eddie said quietly as he descended through the floor.

"Why, you . . ." were McCobber's parting words, and the light from Eddie's candle was lost behind the closing door.

The raven chuckled softly, then cocked his head and listened. Leaves rustled outside the window. Pushing off, the raven caught the tail of a breeze that carried him into the night.

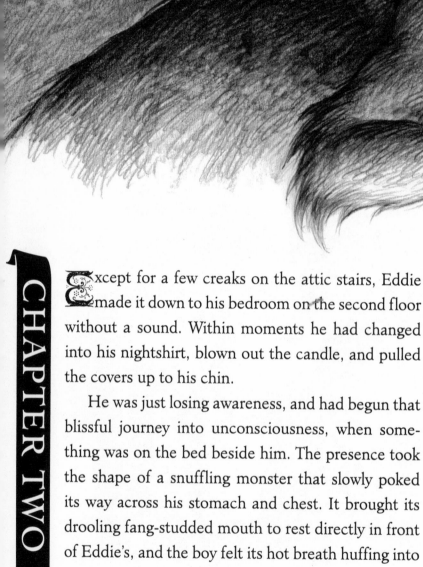

CHAPTER TWO

Except for a few creaks on the attic stairs, Eddie made it down to his bedroom on the second floor without a sound. Within moments he had changed into his nightshirt, blown out the candle, and pulled the covers up to his chin.

He was just losing awareness, and had begun that blissful journey into unconsciousness, when something was on the bed beside him. The presence took the shape of a snuffling monster that slowly poked its way across his stomach and chest. It brought its drooling fang-studded mouth to rest directly in front of Eddie's, and the boy felt its hot breath huffing into his very own nostrils. Trying to cry out, fear strangled him, and his eyes shot open.

"Cairo!" Eddie cried. A large black cat, significantly less terrifying than the monster his mind had imagined, nestled on the boy's chest, purring in his face.

"For cryin' out loud," McCobber gasped. "What's the beast tryin' to do, suck the very life out of us?"

Kneading contentedly, the cat dug his needle-sharp claws into Eddie's chest.

"Not tonight, buddy," Eddie said, lifting the sheet in a way that encouraged the cat to leave the bed. Cairo grudgingly jumped to the floor. The boy rolled over, pulling the covers even higher, and buried his sleepy head into the pillow.

Cairo lazily sauntered to the open window, leapt to the sill, and began grooming himself in the moonlight. Exhausted, Eddie was soon stepping over the threshold into the heavenly realm of sleep—when the cat gave vent to a guttural yowl that surely must have had its origins in the bowels of hell.

"Cairo!" he cried in a loud whisper. "Stop that!" The cat answered with another unearthly wail.

"Yikes," McCobber sputtered, half-asleep. "He sounds like my uncle Craven when he drowned in that bucket of holy water." He shuddered, and grumpily nestled deeper into the folds of Eddie's nightshirt.

Cairo seemed to enjoy the sound of his own voice and let loose with another bloodcurdling yowl.

"Arrgh!" McCobber growled. "Can't you do something?"

Eddie grabbed his pillow and tossed it in the cat's general direction. He had hoped that it would at least frighten the animal away. But with annoying calm Cairo watched as the pillow plopped unthreateningly beside him on the sill. There it balanced for a moment, before teetering through the half-open window and tumbling to the earth below.

Silhouetted against the stars, the black cat stood, stretched, and with apparent ease leapt from the window ledge to a tree branch that grew within easy reach, just outside. There, amidst the branches and at his leisure, he resumed licking his paws.

A moment later another hideous yowl tore the silence. Driven to more drastic measures, Eddie hurled one of his shoes. It struck the windowpane with a bang and fell noisily to the floor.

"Cripes!" McCobber flinched. "I don't know who's worse—that creature or you, you clattering savage!"

But it seemed to have worked, for the momentary hush lingered and then stretched into a restful silence. Eddie tried not to mourn the loss of his only pillow, and curled his arm under his head. He was just drifting off when a slightly more distant yowl assaulted him through the open window. It was followed quickly by another.

Springing from his bed, he made a loud whispered "PSSST" sound in the cat's general direction, then slammed down the window sash. The yowls were still audible when he returned to his bed, so he turned his back to the window and pulled the covers over his head.

Against all odds Eddie entered dreamland. Clad

in armor and out of breath, he stood looking into the dark forest. He could hear the distant caterwauling of a giant panther beast that he had just forced to retreat into the misty wood.

Behind him, and against a dawning sky, rose a grassy knoll onto which he now walked. Removing his helmet, he was suddenly aware of how exhausted he truly was. His knees buckled, and he sank into the lush green grass. Softly the blades moved, and rising to meet him, they transformed themselves into a bed of flowers. Four graceful trees sprouted and grew at the corners. Beautiful sylphs and fairies arrived, carried on a summer breeze. They loosened his straps and gently removed his armor. The trees continued growing until their leafy branches arched in a living canopy overhead. Then a cloud of sprites, trailing a flowing banner of gossamer, bedecked the outstretched boughs.

Within these curtains, and stretched upon this fairy bed, Sir Edgar took his ease. A wood nymph was offering him a peeled grape when a horrendous crowing split the air.

Fairy folk rushed past him, and a gigantic rooster-like head thrust itself through the curtains and towered above him. It was a fabulous creature known as a cockatrice—half-rooster, half-serpent. But this monstrosity was not of the common barnyard variety. This was a death-dealing giant. In an instant its bird-quick eye caught sight of the pile of shining armor. Both Edgar and the monster lunged for the weapons, but the cockatrice was faster. Horrified, the brave

knight watched the huge beak shatter and devour his enchanted sword, piece by piece.

The cockatrice took one final gulp, and the sword disappeared down the monstrous gullet as the fiend reared back, preparing to strike. As it did so, the gossamer curtains caught on its neck and comb. Ripped from its fairy moorings, the delicate fabric cascaded to the ground. The cockatrice emitted another horrific crow, this time spewing jagged pieces of broken sword down onto Sir Edgar, who winced behind his upheld shield as the ricocheting shards bit into any unprotected flesh. The knight had no choice but to retreat.

Suddenly from behind him the giant panther beast emerged, yowling, from the forest. Through white dagger-size fangs it snarled and hissed as it made its way into the clearing. Edgar was trapped between the

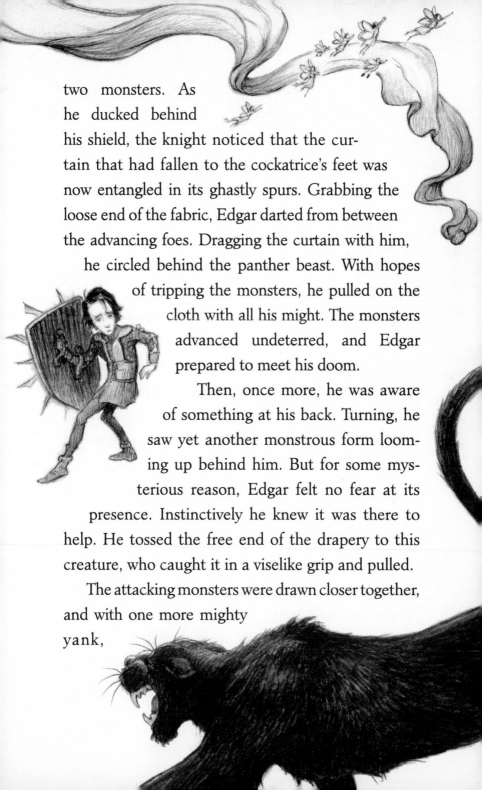

two monsters. As
he ducked behind
his shield, the knight noticed that the curtain that had fallen to the cockatrice's feet was
now entangled in its ghastly spurs. Grabbing the
loose end of the fabric, Edgar darted from between
the advancing foes. Dragging the curtain with him,
he circled behind the panther beast. With hopes
of tripping the monsters, he pulled on the
cloth with all his might. The monsters
advanced undeterred, and Edgar
prepared to meet his doom.

Then, once more, he was aware
of something at his back. Turning, he
saw yet another monstrous form loom-
ing up behind him. But for some mysterious reason, Edgar felt no fear at its
presence. Instinctively he knew it was there to
help. He tossed the free end of the drapery to this
creature, who caught it in a viselike grip and pulled.

The attacking monsters were drawn closer together,
and with one more mighty
yank,

they were pulled face to snarling face. Suddenly the monsters' anger was directed at each other and they began to fight. With amazing speed the friendly creature began to encircle and entwine them in the ever-tightening cloth. Soon the two monsters had become one in a writhing cocoon of screams and yowls.

Slinging the hissing, squawking bundle over its shoulder, the friendly creature turned and gave Edgar a "tip of the hat" gesture.

"Farewell, and thank you!" The knight waved as the creature nimbly scaled an ancient tower that had risen out of the mist. Atop this tower stood a gallows-like structure, from which the creature hung the monstrous bundle. With a final wave the mysterious being vanished, leaving the squalling twosome suspended betwixt heaven and earth.

Edgar was still gazing upward when he became aware of shouting voices that soon grew louder than even those of the battling monsters. He assumed it must be the happy villagers, who, realizing the danger that was now past, were coming out of hiding to hail him as their hero.

He was preparing to receive their boundless appreciation when he realized that the shouts were not of joy but of anger.

Eddie was also aware that his bare feet were cold and wet with dew. He shivered and awakened, to find himself dressed in his nightshirt and standing in the neighbor's poultry yard. Chickens of all sizes and descriptions ran back and forth in terror. Behind him the gate to the yard stood open as escaped chickens strutted or mingled together on the dewy lawn.

The shouting became understandable. "What are you doing to my chickens, you scoundrel?" Eddie was trying to make sense of it all when he realized it was his neighbor Judge Washington who was shouting. The judge, also dressed in a nightshirt, was waving a cane as he stormed off his porch and across the lawn toward Eddie. He was also gesturing violently in the

direction of his barn roof. "And what in the name of the devil have you done to my prized rooster?" he shouted.

There, at the very peak of the barn roof, hanging from the weather vane was what appeared to be a white cloth sack, which was filled with something alive and something very angry that wanted to get out. Eddie then realized yet another thing: The one constant element that had not changed or stopped, the thing that was the same in his dream and in real time, was the sound of enraged shrieks and caterwauling, and those sounds were coming from that sack.

"Oh, boy-o!" McCobber whispered warily. "It looks like we've done it this time!"

A hand seized Eddie by the collar and yanked him

nearly off his feet. "I don't know what you were up to, boy," the judge scolded, "but I'll see justice done!"

"Ruby!" he called to his servant as he half-dragged, half-carried Eddie out of the poultry yard and onto the lawn. "Ruby, you gather these chickens before they run off into the next county!"

"Titus, you and the others fetch the ladder and bring down that wretched sack! And you . . ." The judge was again turning his attention and wrath on Eddie.

At that moment John Allan's bedroom window flew open and the man's head and shoulders leaned into the dawn's unfolding drama.

"Judge! Eddie? . . . What the . . . ?"

"ALLAN!" the judge shouted, holding Eddie out in front of him, as if the boy were Exhibit A. "This no-account orphan of yours has gone too far this time!"

"Aye, now. Hold on, Judge." Even Allan's firm Scottish accent sounded a bit shaken. "I'll be right down. Just hold on . . ." He disappeared back into the house.

A familiar cawing was heard,

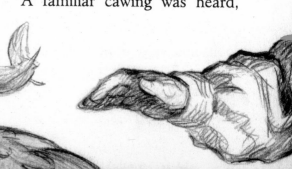

and Eddie looked up to see the raven circling
overhead.

"Acch!" muttered McCobber. "I'll never
hear the end of
this one!"

Still clutching Eddie's collar, the judge shouted orders to his servants and punctuated each command with a bone-jarring shake.

"Now, Judge, what's all this?" John Allan was tying shut his robe as he hastened across the backyard of his house.

"Can't you see?" the judge fumed. "Your boy here broke into my chicken yard, scattered all my hens, and stole my prize rooster!"

"Edgar," Allan asked, "is this true?"

"I . . . I don't know, sir," Eddie tried to explain. "One minute I was asleep, and the next thing I know I'm down here in the hen yard—"

"You see?" barked the judge. "He's confessed!"

Their attention was drawn to the servants trying to rescue the sack. A long ladder leaned against the barn as one servant stood at its base and another at its top, and a third man straddled the peak, making his way toward the weather vane.

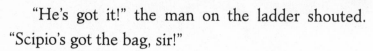

CHAPTER THREE

"He's got it!" the man on the ladder shouted. "Scipio's got the bag, sir!"

There had been a momentary lull in the hissing and squabbling from the bag, but it renewed in full vigor as Scipio inched his way back across the wooden shingles. At last the unhappy package was delivered to the master of the house.

"Well, open it up!" he commanded as they laid it at his feet.

"Don't just stand there. Let the poor thing out!"

The knot in the sack proved too tight, so Scipio produced a penknife and cut the bag open. Instantly the battered rooster appeared in a flurry of his own swirling feathers. Dazed, angry, and panic-stricken, the bird ran into the yard.

A second later another form shot out of the bag. A jet-black thing dashed toward the Allans' house. Stopping about halfway, it looked back wild-eyed before tearing into the bushes.

"By thunder!" cried Allan. "That's Cairo, our cat!"

"I tell you, Allan," the judge began with renewed anger, "the boy is no good! Leave him to me and I'll whip some sense into him!" Just as he raised his arm

to strike Eddie, the raven swooped, flapping its wings momentarily in the man's face.

"By God!" the judge backed away as the raven flew to the henhouse roof, cawing. "And I'll ring that devil's neck!" the man cried.

"Now, now . . ." Allan tried to calm his neighbor. "You needn't worry," he said, as he reached out and pulled Eddie toward him. "I'll make him sorry he did this."

"See to it!" the judge threatened. "And mark my words, Allan, if that rooster is spoiled, I'll see you in front of my own bench!"

"I understand, Judge," Allan reassured him. "We bear the full responsibility here. Just let me know what this insolence has set you back, and we will pay it."

"Excuse me, Master Allan." It was the deep voice of Allan's butler, Dap. He too joined the little crowd in the yard. "Master Allan, sir, I beg your pardon, but it just doesn't seem likely that young Master Eddie could have climbed all the way up on that roof and then back down here without a ladder."

"Why," the judge spat, "such insolence!"

"He does have a point, your honor," Allan agreed. "It took three of your men with a ladder a good fifteen minutes to fetch that sack down here."

"Well," replied the judge, a bit flustered. "Well, he must have thrown it up there."

Dap silently looked at Eddie, then to the barn, across the roof, and up to the cupola on which the weather vane stood. It was obvious to everyone, even the judge, that his suggestion seemed very unlikely, if not impossible.

At that moment the raven swooped down and landed on Eddie's shoulder.

"Why, that's it," the judge cried. "He must have had that infernal bird carry it up there!"

"He's strong, Judge," Eddie spoke up, "but I don't think even he could carry a bag with a fighting cat and rooster in it all the way to the top of that roof."

"Explain this, then!" the judge tossed the remnants of the tattered bag at the boy.

It appeared to be a pillowcase. In script along its cuff the initials *JA* were elegantly embroidered. A sick wave washed over Eddie as he remembered the pillow he had thrown at Cairo the night before— the pillow that had fallen out the window.

Allan took the case, running the embroidery through his own fingers. "Why, it's one of ours!"

"Well, Mr. Allan," the judge replied with a smug tilt of his chin, "I believe I rest my case."

CHAPTER FOUR

Up in his bedroom Eddie was changing into his school clothes. McCobber waited on the rim of the washbasin that sat on the dresser, and the raven spoke from the foot of the bed.

"I leave you two alone for a few hours, and look what happens," the raven said, exasperated.

"Don't blame me!" McCobber bleated. "I didn't do anything!"

"Oh, noooo, you never do anything," the raven said. "You just egg him on, that's all! Putting thoughts into his head—encouraging him!"

"I just suggested we get rid of that filthy cat so we could get a little sleep, that's all," McCobber cried. "The next thing I know, someone's run old Yowl and Cluck up the flagpole, and the place is in an uproar."

"Don't play innocent with me, you little fiend," the raven continued. "Why, you'd push your she-devil grandmother down a well just for the fun of hearing her splash."

"You leave my grandmother out of this!" McCobber fumed, hovering in wing-flapping anger. "Besides, you're not off the hook yourself. For all I know you might just be in on it, you old carcass picker!" the imp cried, shaking his fist.

"All right, that's enough—both of you!" Eddie had been pacing while buttoning his shirt. He stopped and pounded his chest. "Are you trying to drive me

mad? I'm the one who's doomed to the lash. I'm the one in torment! And the worst part is, I think I may have done it!"

Realizing he was right, the pair grudgingly postponed their ongoing spat.

"Dap made a great point, you know," the raven said, trying to offer some encouragement. "There is no way you could have gotten that bag onto the roof without a ladder or a pair of wings."

"And that's where you come in." McCobber sneered.

"It wasn't me," the raven said, turning on the imp. "I *know* what *I* was doing before all the ruckus. It's you two who can't seem to account for yourselves!"

"It's like I said out there," Eddie said. "I was asleep, dreaming, and then—"

"And what were you dreaming?" the raven asked.

"That I was a knight," Eddie began, "a knight fighting a . . . a . . ."

"Yeah," the raven encouraged, "go on. Fighting what?"

"A giant yowling cat and a hideous crowing cockatrice!" Eddie cried in despair as he sunk onto his bed, clutching his head in his hands.

"Oh, yeah." McCobber's eyes lit up. "That was a good one if I do say so myself!"

"I thought you said you didn't have anything to do with this?" The raven's voice hit an accusing note.

McCobber suddenly grew sheepish. "Well, just a suggestion or two."

The raven turned back to the boy. "Now, Eddie. Think. Did you stick Cairo and that rooster into your pillowcase?"

"I don't know!" Eddie cried in agony. "That's just it. I don't know!"

"All right, all right, take it easy," the raven said. "Okay, Mac, what about you? You were there too. Did he actually go through the motions of catching those critters and hanging them from the weather vane?"

McCobber shrugged helplessly.

"You guys drive me nuts!" the raven said, losing his patience. "Can't you tell a dream from reality? Don't you know where one ends and the other begins?"

There was a soft rapping at the bedroom door, and everyone fell silent.

"Y-yes?" Eddie asked. "Who is it?"

"It's me, Dap, Master Eddie. Your presence is requested at the breakfast table."

"Oh, Dap!" Eddie flung open the door in relief, and was so happy to see his old friend smiling from the other side, he nearly started to cry. "Oh, Dap, what am I going to do? Everyone thinks I did this cruel thing, and I'm sure to get a whipping for it!"

"Master Allan is a hard man, that's true enough," Dap offered, "but he is also a fair man. It seems to me if you use logic with him, he's bound to see the truth."

"Which is . . . ?" Eddie asked.

"Now, Master Eddie," Dap said, "you know you didn't do it. Common sense must tell you that."

"But I dreamt—," Eddie started.

"Dreamin' and doin' are two different things," Dap said, and smiled. "And no one—I don't care how much brainpower he's got—has ever dreamt a sack full of a fighting rooster and cat to the top of a barn roof."

"But someone put it up there," Eddie said.

"Now, that *is* a fact," Dap replied. "Maybe if you start from there and go about asking the right questions . . ."

"You mean, I'm supposed to find out who did this before I go down there and get a whippin'?" Eddie was incredulous. "That's impossible!"

"Whether they whip you or not isn't what's important, Master Eddie," Dap said.

"Maybe not to *you*," Eddie said, feeling as if no one cared what happened to him. "It's not your hide going under the lash." Eddie's voice was full of indignant self-pity, and he looked to Dap, expecting an apology. The man merely met his gaze, and without saying a word his old eyes spoke eloquently of a lifetime filled with unjust whipping and unfair punishment.

The boy winced and started to speak, but Dap held up his hand, silencing him. "Like I said, Master Eddie," he continued, "whether they whip you or not is not what is important. What's important is that one person knows the truth."

Eddie shrugged in response. "Yeah, and who might that be?"

"Why, young Edgar Poe," Dap said. "That's who."

CHAPTER FIVE

As Eddie and Dap walked down the hall toward the staircase, Eddie imagined himself a doomed prisoner being escorted to his execution. Dap had become his father confessor, the one appointed to accompany the condemned as he walked "the last mile."

Soft carpet, delicate wallpaper, and warm woodwork mutated into cold, hard, slime-covered walls that made up a dank torch-lit passageway. Out of the shadows stepped two tall, hooded figures: one carried a double-edged axe, the other a cat-o'-nine-tails. Grimly they began the descent of the stone spiral stairway that coiled downward into the bowels of utter darkness.

Ahead, unknown horrors awaited. Eddie shuddered. The agonizing anticipation twisted his guts and squirmed in his chest, forcing him to gasp for breath. He alone could hear the panic-choked voice of McCobber raving in his ear. "They can't do this to us! I'm innocent, I tell ya. INNOCENT! You gotta save me! SAVE ME!" On and on he went.

Halfway down the stairs Dab turned, speaking quietly. "Remember, Master Eddie, everyone has only seen this thing from one angle, and from that point of view, you *look* guilty. What you have to keep in mind is that this world is full of angles, and one of them is bound to lead you to a place with a better view." He smiled.

Eddie blinked and answered as if awakening from a dream, "Uh . . . what?"

"I said, you've got to open their eyes." Dap put his hand on the boy's shoulder, and Eddie looked into his smiling face. The hopeless dark passage was engulfed in warmth, as sunlight now flooded the stairwell. "You've got to show them what we already know— that you are innocent."

Eddie smiled back. The entryway of the Allan home seemed to sparkle in the sunshine as they descended the remaining stairs and walked through the front hall. At the partially closed dining room door, the two friends paused once again.

"Thanks, Dap," Eddie whispered. "Wish me luck."

Dap tapped himself on the temple. "Just use your head, boy." He smiled broadly and winked before turning to continue noiselessly down the hall to the kitchen.

"And you," Eddie, under his breath, warned the demon on his shoulder, "shut. Up." He then took a deep breath and pushed open the dining room door.

Although the room was awash with warm morning sunlight, there was an ominous silence that cast a cold shadow over the breakfast table. John Allan sat at one end, reading a newspaper, and Fannie, his wife, sat at the other. Eddie slipped quietly into his chair, trying not to be noticed. Fannie looked up, her eyes red. Apparently she had been crying. Master Allan's eyes barely left his newspaper.

Eddie entertained the feeble hope that if he simply acted as if nothing were wrong, the whole thing would just go away. As he helped himself to some scrambled eggs, the light clink of silverware against porcelain was the only sound to break the heavy stillness. But even that seemed to draw too much attention his way, so after putting just one small scoop onto his plate,

he noiselessly eased the spoon back into the serving bowl and left it there. That was all right. He wasn't hungry anyway. He kept his head down as he pretended to eat and concentrated on being invisible.

Eddie had been so young when he'd come to live with the Allans that his memories of it now were foggy. But in his mind one thing always remained crystal clear: They had taken him in when he'd had nowhere else to go. They had welcomed him into their home and treated him well. He had even come to call them Ma and Pa. And yet . . .

"Edgar." John Allan's voice cut through the silence, seeming louder than it truly was. Startled, Eddie felt his stomach tighten.

"Edgar, your ma and I are just about at wit's end!"

So much for this whole thing just going away.

"Pa." Eddie cleared his throat and sat forward in his chair, trying to meet his foster father's hawklike gaze. "I know it didn't look good out there this morning, but you have to believe me, I didn't do anything wrong."

"Oh, Eddie!" Fannie cried softly into her napkin and turned away.

Eddie felt as if the wind had been knocked out of him. He'd known he'd have to prove himself to John Allan—he was *always* having to prove himself to John Allan—but Ma? If anybody had ever believed in him, it was Fannie. Her doubt blindsided him, and he slumped back in his chair.

"Haven't we done enough for you?" Allan's flinty Scottish accent was arrowhead sharp. "A good home, nice clothes, fine schools . . . and how do you repay us?"

Eddie slumped deeper into his chair and lowered

his head. Usually he and the Allans tried to pretend that they were a happy little family: father, mother, and son. But today, at this moment, that all seemed a million miles away. Edgar was not their son. Edgar would never be their son. The growing differences between him and John Allan seemed to become more and more painfully obvious every day.

"All you want to do is skulk around in that attic, root through Uncle Galt's rubbish, and scribble till all hours. Moody insolence is one thing, but stupid pranks and now *lying*! That's another! And I tell you, lad, I WON'T HAVE IT!" He slammed his fist onto the table. Plates, silverware, and the other two people present jumped.

Eddie, and even Fannie, cowered. He had seen Pa angry before. In fact, Pa always seemed vaguely annoyed, but this anger was more intense. Was this it, then? Was this the day Pa would finally throw Eddie out?

"I know now that I have been too soft with you! In the past your ma has always managed to stay my hand, but not today. This time a good thrashing is what you'll get!"

A sob caught in Fannie's throat. Eddie's head dropped even lower as he tried to hide his face. The unfairness of it all made him so angry, he thought he would cry, and the last thing he wanted John Allan to see him do now was cry.

"It's not that I want to do it, lad." Allan's tone softened a little. "But you leave me no choice. It's the only way to wake you up, and you've got to wake up, boy. You can't spend the rest of your life dreaming of greatness and pretending to be a poet. You've got to get your head out of the clouds and keep your feet on the ground. Pull yourself up by your bootstraps like I had to do!"

"Pulled himself up by his own bootstraps . . . Baa!" McCobber growled sarcastically. "Why, whenever this jerk has gotten himself in over his head, he's had rich old Uncle Galt to pull his Highland bacon out of the fire!" Eddie smiled in secret agreement but said nothing.

"Ah, poetry's all right, lad," Allan continued. "I'm fond of the rhymes myself, but in their place." Eddie thought Pa now sounded like the minister on Sunday morning, who, once he had shoveled in the fire and brimstone, went on to offer a chance at salvation. "Show me a poem with some moral fiber and common sense to it, and I'll show you a thing of value. Have you never heard the old saying 'No man e'er was glorious / Who was not laborious'? Now, that's poetry—truly words to live by."

"But I do labor," Eddie interjected. He alone knew how hard he worked on his writing, and he wasn't going to sit there and let John Allan infer that he was lazy. "I work every night."

"But to what end—and at what price?" Allan asked. "Remember, 'Early to bed and early to rise makes a man healthy, wealthy, and wise.' That's another poem you should commit to memory."

Eddie rolled his eyes and sighed.

"So practicality isn't good enough for you, ay?" Allan's temper was rising again. "The wisdom that comes from an honest day's work is beneath you, is it? Well, it's practical thinking and hard work that's put a roof over your head, not moonin' around memorizing the plays of Shakespeare! That will only get you poverty and leave you in need of charity, just like your destitute parents before you!"

"You, sir, have crossed a line!" Before Eddie realized what was happening, he was on his feet. Anger coursed through him like an electric current and propelled him out of his chair. Allan had cornered him like a homeless dog and beaten him down with guilt and shame, but the man should not have poked this stray with that particular stick. The hair stood high on the back of his neck as he tried to catch his breath and find his words.

"I don't care what you think about me. You can tell me I'm . . . I'm ungrateful . . . and . . . I'm . . . a . . . fool. And you can sit there and accuse me of a million stupid things. But don't you ever—EVER—try to smear my mother's name."

If John Allan had been another kid in the school yard, Eddie would have blackened his eye right about now. As it was, he could only stand there facing the man across the breakfast table—fists clenched, chest heaving and trembling with barely contained rage.

Allan eyed him, unflinching,

and in a firm no-nonsense tone responded. "Edgar, I will not let this discussion go off course. We will not waste time bandying words over any matter other than the one at hand, and that is—your responsibility for the fracas this morning!"

"So my guilt has been decided, then." Eddie returned the iron stare. His breathing was back to normal but his heart was still pounding. He remained standing.

"It seems that that would be the logical conclusion, yes," Allan answered. "You were found at the scene, the animals were in your pillowcase, and when questioned, you could not deny it."

"I tell you, I must have been sleepwalking." Eddie knew that sounded lame, but it was the truth, and that was all he had. "The last thing I remember before hearing the judge shout was a dream I was having."

"Perhaps," Allan said grimly, "your dreams led you to commit a dark act."

"You speak of logic," Eddie countered, feeling his words returning to him, "and yet does logic tell you that I could have dreamt a sack full of writhing creatures to suspend themselves from the highest point in the neighborhood?"

"I'll grant you," Allan admitted, "where they were found does cast the biggest doubt on your guilt."

"The biggest, perhaps, but not the *only* doubt." Eddie felt another current racing through him now— not a surge of all-consuming rage but the power of language and logic. He had found his footing and was off and running. He began his defense.

"First of all, who in this entire household cares most for old Cairo? Who feeds and tends to him? Me, that's who. And yet, who in this household—and perhaps the whole neighborhood, for that matter—has not been annoyed by his midnight yowling? Why, just the other night, did you not yourself throw a slipper at him?"

Allan cleared his throat, and Fannie piped in, "He is right. He *has* always been kind to animals."

"And who in this household," Eddie resumed, "or in this neighborhood has not been ripped from sweet slumber by the predawn crowing of that fiendish fowl? Who within earshot has not dreamt of seeing that wretched rooster simmering in a stew pot?"

"Easy," McCobber whispered. "Easy, boy."

Eddie continued, "And who in the neighborhood can do a thing about it? A bird like that shouldn't be allowed to crow before sunrise within the city limits! But that fowl happens to be the prize rooster of a very powerful judge, so the good folk suffer, and the cock crows on!"

"So you took matters into your own hands," Allan said.

"Someone did," Eddie answered.

"The circumstantial evidence points to you."

"But suspicion falls on anyone within the sound of that hellish cock-a-doodle-doo!"

"So what would you have me do?" Allan asked. "Put the neighborhood on trial to spare you a whipping?"

"Give me two days," Eddie said. "Two days to find the culprit and clear my name."

Allan shook his head. "I am afraid the judge will want to see justice meted out more swiftly than that."

"Who is master in this house?" Eddie asked. "Judge Washington or John Allan?"

"Oooh." McCobber chuckled. "Nice one."

Allan eyed him steadily in silence. "I shall give you one day. If in twenty-four hours you cannot show me evidence of your innocence, you will be punished. Understood?"

"Yes, sir." Eddie nodded. "Thank you, sir."

"Now," Allan said, resuming his newspaper, "you'd better eat your breakfast and get ready for school."

"If you don't mind, sir"—Eddie remained standing—"I haven't much of an appetite, and I thought I could use these eggs to try to coax Cairo out of the bushes. I'm afraid that rooster might have actually done him some harm."

Allan nodded, and as Eddie picked up his plate and headed to the kitchen, Fannie squeezed his hand. "I believe you, Eddie," she said. "Good luck."

CHAPTER SIX

ddie nearly collapsed as the kitchen door swung
shut behind him.

"A reprieve!" McCobber chortled. "Thank heaven,
a reprieve!"

Dap's friendly hand patted his shoulder. He and
the cook were both brimming over with contained
laughter. "Congratulations, boy!" Hattie the cook
surrounded him with a big hug, and Eddie's head was
swimming with the scent of freshly laundered uni-
form and melted butter.

"Why, I ain't never seen anyone in this house
stand up to old Master John like that before! That
was fine, mighty fine!" She laughed again.

Like a victorious boxer who has just stepped out of the ring, Eddie was dazed but happy.

"I knew you could do it!" Dap beamed proudly.

"I still have to find out who really did it," Eddie reminded him.

"Just use your head," Dap said as he tapped his temple, "and you'll do fine!"

Eddie walked out the back door feeling like a new man. As the morning sun warmed his face, he inhaled deeply. The crisp autumn air was like a heavy perfume. The screen door slammed behind him, and he practically danced down the porch steps and into the side yard. He stopped at the large overgrown bushes along the side of the house. This was about where Cairo had disappeared earlier that morning.

"Cairo, breakfast," he called softly. A pitiful mew replied from somewhere in the shrubbery.

Getting down on his hands and knees, Eddie peered beneath the largest bush. His nostrils filled with the musty smell of damp earth and growing things. Huddled in the back, close to the house, was the familiar silhouette of Cairo, his green eyes catching the filtered sunlight.

"Ah, there's the old troublemaker," McCobber whispered. "Careful he doesn't try to rip out your throat."

"Come on, buddy," Eddie coached. "Time for breakfast."

Within the motionless black cutout of the cat's form, green eyes blinked slowly.

"Come oonn. It's your favorite." Eddie's fingernail tapped the china plate, making a soft dinging sound. "Scrambled eggs." Gingerly the old cat emerged.

"Here you go, Cairo." Eddie placed the plate in the grass within a few feet of the cat, who stretched and stiffly walked over to Eddie and rubbed against his leg. Then, purring loudly, the cat began to gobble down the eggs.

Eddie stroked Cairo's disheveled coat. There were patches of missing fur and a few cuts, but nothing too serious. "It doesn't look too bad, Cairo. At least we're still friends." The animal's trust further bolstered the boy's spirits. "Don't worry. We'll find out who did this to you."

Just then the raven landed on Eddie's shoulder. "How'd it go in there?" he asked.

"We got out of it!" McCobber beamed. "Nobody's gonna whip my boy today!"

"Really?" The raven was delighted, yet skeptical.

"Well," Eddie said, petting Cairo, "that's half-true. He's given me twenty-four hours to prove I'm innocent, before he beats me."

"Ah, yes." The raven smiled. "We can always count on our friend the imp for half-truths." McCobber made a face. "So, what are you going to do now?" asked the raven.

"Well, I wanted to make sure that Cairo was okay, first." Eddie rose to his feet. "After that, I wasn't exactly sure . . ." Looking across the yard, he saw his pillow lying in the grass. "I guess that's as good a place to start as any." He walked over and picked it up.

From there he could see the path he must have taken a few hours before. His footprints were still visible in the dewy grass. They came from around the front of the house, stopped there at the pillow, and then continued toward the chicken yard and henhouse.

"This doesn't look too good." McCobber sighed.

"How about a new rule?" the raven suggested. "If you don't have anything positive to say, then just SHUT UP!"

Retracing his steps, Eddie followed them to the poultry yard fence. Inside, the chickens seemed to be clucking and scratching as usual. Then he noticed the rooster. Hiding under half of an old, broken barrel, he looked nervously out every few seconds.

As a hen and her brood passed, a curious chick stopped and peeped into the shadow beneath the barrel. Fearing for his life, the panic-stricken rooster dashed for the safety of the henhouse. His once proud plumage was all disheveled, and large patches of white featherless skin dappled his scrawny body.

Eddie felt something he never would have guessed he could have felt: pity, for that boisterous old bird.

He looked at the buildings surrounding the yard. Across the alley stood Murphy's boardinghouse, and behind him, the Allans'. On his immediate right was the henhouse and yard, and beyond that, the judge's house and barn.

It had all been so dark the night before, he thought, when he had looked at the same scene from the attic window. But wait—it hadn't been *all* dark. There had been a light burning in the window of the back room of the boardinghouse! Someone else had been up as

late as he was, and maybe someone else had been trying to get to sleep when the cock crowed!

"Get away from there!" the judge shouted from
the house. "Haven't you done enough damage for
one day?!"

"Sorry, Judge," Eddie jumbled. "I . . . ah . . . was
just paying my respects."

"You'll pay, boy!" the judge was coming out his
back door. "YOU'LL PAY."

"Sorry, sir." Eddie bowed and started running. "I'd
like to stay, but I fear I'll be late for school." With that,
he disappeared around the corner of the house, leaving the judge to shake his cane in wrathful solitude.

ddie's school day was a constant reminder of the troubles that he hoped he had left at home. It started in history class, where they studied the horrifying days of the Spanish Inquisition. All the talk of torture and interrogation only served to stoke the fires of McCobber's imagination, leading him to wonder aloud which would be worse—to be slowly stretched to death on the rack, or enclosed in the spike-lined embrace of the iron maiden.

Literature, usually Eddie's favorite subject, was even worse. Today's topic: the themes of heaven and

hell in poetry. They touched on Dante's poem *The Inferno*. Its descriptions of the damned, suffering the pains of eternal punishment, actually seemed like light reading compared to the unspeakable fate that awaited Eddie if he couldn't prove himself innocent. Or at least that was McCobber's opinion.

Their teacher also summarized John Milton's *Paradise Lost*. But Adam and Eve's banishment from Eden seemed somewhat trivial considering Eddie's plight. The teacher was reading some passages aloud when he came to Satan's line, "Better to reign in Hell than serve in Heaven." McCobber cheered lustily in Eddie's ear and stamped his clawlike feet.

"That Satan," McCobber hooted, "What a riot!"

At long last the day was over, and Eddie headed without delay to the house in which the only other light in the neighborhood burned the night before.

MURPHY'S BOARDINGHOUSE
ROOMS TO LET
NO PETS ALLOWED

Eddie could read the sign from the sidewalk out front. Determined to get information, he pulled a pad and pencil from his book satchel, mounted the stairs, and knocked. A gray-haired woman answered. Although Eddie had rarely spoken with her, he recognized her immediately as the proprietor.

"Mrs. Murphy, I presume," Eddie said, and smiled. He would have tipped his hat if he had worn one.

"I am here to offer you and everyone in your household a ten-day free trial of the award-winning *Richmond Enquirer* newspaper. That's right, ten days of our wonderful newspaper absolutely free! Would you like to take advantage of this limited-time offer?"

The woman was pleasantly surprised. "Why, yes," she said, eyes glistening greedily. "We would like to get the paper for free."

"Wonderful!" Eddie lifted his pad and prepared to write. "Now, if I could have the names of all the residents, please."

Mrs. Murphy eyed him skeptically. "What do you need to know that for?"

"Simply a formality, madam," he answered. "We would like to make sure that each and every resident receives the free paper they are entitled to."

"Well, all right." She seemed satisfied. "Let's see. There's Mrs. Holmeburger in the front room, the Olsons across the hall, Miss Wiggam, and then Captain Mephisto."

"Very good." Eddie jotted happily. "Now, this Captain Mephisto. Is his room at the back corner of the house on this side?"

"Yeess." Mrs. Murphy's suspicion had returned. "But why is that important?"

"Just giving our delivery boy as much information as possible, ma'am." He smiled and continued scrawling in the pad. "Now one last question and I will be on my way. Does anyone in the house have any pets—like, say, a raccoon or perhaps a baboon?"

"Young man!" Mrs. Murphy stood up straight and pointed to her sign. "Can't you read? NO PETS—and that's exactly what it means. No pets, no exceptions! Besides, what has that to do with getting the newspaper?" Suddenly a light of recognition shone in her eyes. "Wait a minute. Aren't you that Allan boy? The one who caused all the trouble this morning? What is this, another one of your pranks?"

"Sorry to disturb you, ma'am." Eddie backed away. "And I hope you enjoy the newspaper." Within a few steps he was off the porch and bowing a hasty exit. In a moment he was around the corner of the house and heading down the rutted earthen alley that ran along Mrs. Murphy's property.

As he passed the backyard, Eddie saw a boy about his age pulling weeds. He slowed his pace. Stepping behind a shed that stood in the alley, he stopped. Even the all-seeing eyes of Mrs. Murphy couldn't see him there.

"Psst," he called in a loud whisper. "Hey, kid. Who lives in that room—the one on the corner?"

The boy stood up, leaned on his hoe, and narrowed his eyes. "Who wants to know?"

"Oh, just somebody who might be willing to trade this practically new penknife for a tiny bit of information, that's all." He pulled the knife from his pocket and displayed it temptingly.

The boy looked warily to the house, and then in two quick stealthy steps was in front of Eddie, staring longingly at the knife. Eddie put it into the boy's hand, and the boy smiled at the feel of it. "That would be Captain Mephisto, the magician. That's who lives in that corner room," he said, opening and closing the knife.

"'Magician?'" Eddie asked. "What do you mean by 'magician'?"

"A real magician." The boy's expression was very serious. "He gave some tickets to us and the missus, and we seen him do his show over at the playhouse. He can make gold coins appear out of nowhere, and rabbits and pigeons disappear right before your eyes! But"—he shrugged—"I guess you can do that sort of thing when you're friends with the devil."

"Just because he can do tricks," Eddie said, "doesn't mean he's friends with the devil."

"Oh, it ain't just the tricks." The boy looked over his shoulder, making sure nobody would hear him. "Sometimes . . . late at night, when I walk past his room, I hear him in there talking with the devil . . . and then . . . I hear the devil talkin' back!"

Eddie's eyes widened and he leaned forward. "Really?" Perhaps, he thought, he had more in common with this Mephisto fellow than just staying up late.

"Yeah, yeah." McCobber yawned. "Big deal."

"So, what does this devil sound like?" Eddie asked, intrigued. "What language does it speak?"

"Oh, it's demon language, that's for sure," the boy said. "It's all snarly and snorty and other sounds I don't understand, but when it laughs . . ." He looked

over his shoulder one more time. "It sounds like Satan laughin' on Judgment Day!"

The hair on the back of Eddie's neck stood on end.

"Whoa," McCobber gasped. "I gotta meet this guy!"

Eddie swallowed hard. "If . . . if I came back tonight around midnight, could you let me in?"

"NO WAY!" the boy blurted loudly. Then, remembering himself, he went back to a whisper. "Why, the missus would tan the hide off'n both of us if she caught me doin' somethin' like that. No, sir!" He shook his head to underscore his meaning. "I'd rather

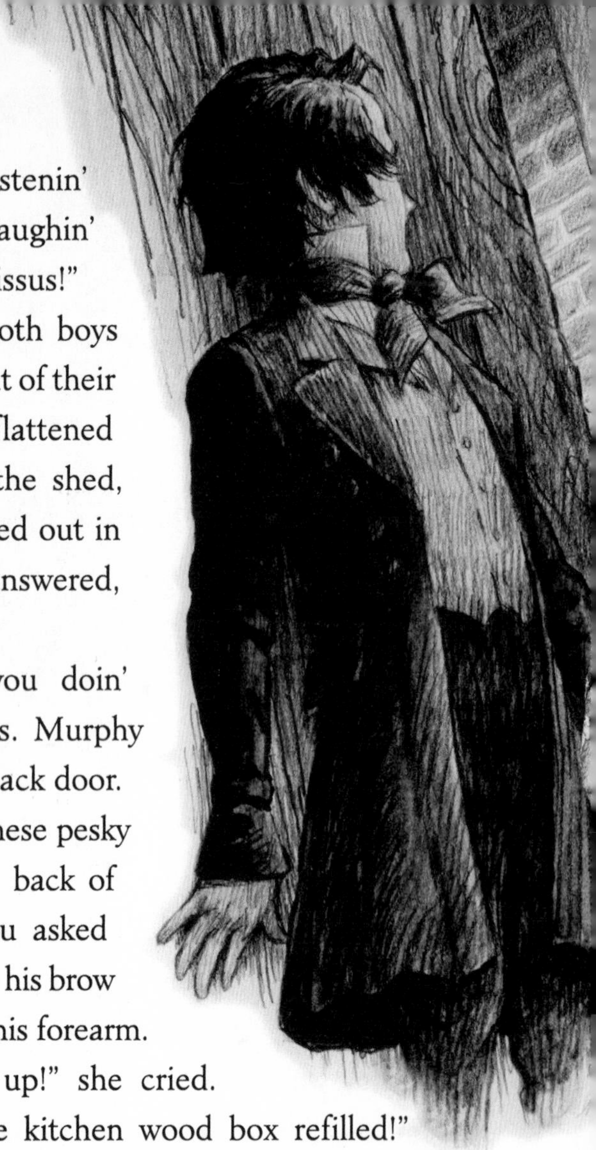

sit up all night listenin'
to that devil laughin'
than cross the missus!"

"ISAIAH!" Both boys
nearly jumped out of their
skins. Eddie flattened
himself against the shed,
and Isaiah stepped out in
plain view and answered,
"Yes, ma'am!"

"What are you doin'
back there?" Mrs. Murphy
called from the back door.

"Just pullin' these pesky
weeds round the back of
the shed like you asked
me to." He wiped his brow
with the back of his forearm.

"Well, hurry up!" she cried.
"Cook needs the kitchen wood box refilled!"

"Yes, ma'am." He bent over, pretended to hoe,
and without looking up whispered to Eddie out of
the corner of his mouth, "I gotta go."

"Wait!" Eddie whispered back. "I have to see that
devil!"

"You might not see the devil," he said as he bent over and picked up the basket full of pulled weeds, "but you can see the man easy enough. He leaves the house every evenin' right after supper and heads to the theater at exactly quarter past seven."

"Thanks, Isaiah," Eddie called softly.

"Thank you." Isaiah smiled and patted the hip pocket that held his new penknife, and then he hurried off toward the house.

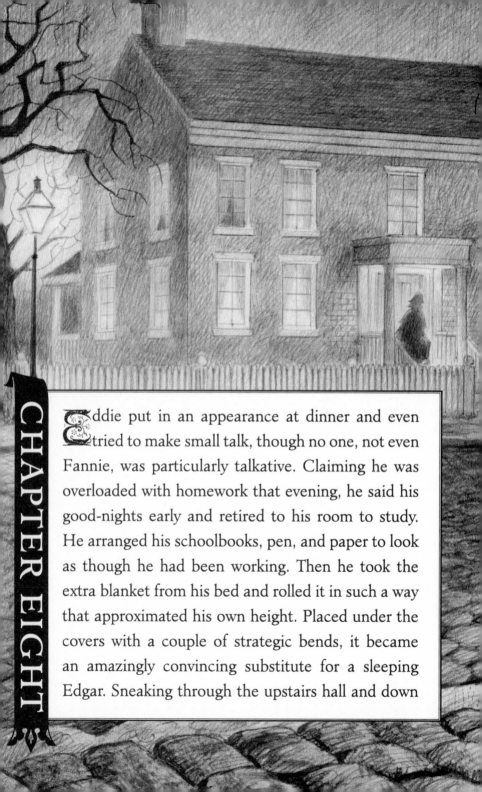

CHAPTER EIGHT

Eddie put in an appearance at dinner and even tried to make small talk, though no one, not even Fannie, was particularly talkative. Claiming he was overloaded with homework that evening, he said his good-nights early and retired to his room to study. He arranged his schoolbooks, pen, and paper to look as though he had been working. Then he took the extra blanket from his bed and rolled it in such a way that approximated his own height. Placed under the covers with a couple of strategic bends, it became an amazingly convincing substitute for a sleeping Edgar. Sneaking through the upstairs hall and down

the back stairs was more of a challenge, but he made it—undetected.

At about fourteen minutes past seven, he was casually strolling across the street from the front of Murphy's boardinghouse. Promptly at seven fifteen a white-bearded gentleman wearing a sea captain's hat and a black inverness cape emerged, carrying a medium-size suitcase.

"Something tells me there's a demon in that luggage," McCobber speculated.

"Or an exotic pet, perhaps," Eddie added.

The man was no more than a step or two down

the porch stairs when a familiar figure appeared in the doorway.

"Excuse me, Captain," she called after him in a very businesslike tone.

"Ah, Mrs. Murphy," Captain Mephisto said before turning around. "So glad you caught me. I was just on my way to the theater when—" As he turned to face her, he was greeted by an outstretched hand. Judging by her stern expression, it was obvious that she was not expecting a hardy handshake.

"Ah, yes." He stopped mid hat-tip. "The rent. I believe I have it right here." With a flourish he set the case on the stair before him and opened it. "Here we go. Just as I thought."

The case was nearly empty, with the exception of a few magicians' props; among them was a small, glittering chest, which he removed. Displaying it in showmanlike fashion, he opened it and looked in. His smile vanished, becoming a perplexed frown. Shrugging, he turned the box upside down . . . Empty.

"Now, this is mysterious," Mephisto said, putting his finger to his chin in thought. "Where do you suppose that rent money has gone? Mrs. Murphy, are you sure I didn't pay you already?"

The landlady grew even more stern, placed her other hand firmly on her hip, and moved her outstretched palm closer to him.

"Why, Mrs. Murphy, I fear you don't believe me." Mephisto laughed nervously. "Or are you simply having fun at my expense?" He reached up and pulled something from behind her left ear. After displaying a gold coin between his thumb and forefinger, he dropped it into her hand and smiled.

Registering only slight surprise, she brought it to her face for closer inspection. Mephisto tipped his hat and started to leave.

"That will be *two* weeks' rent, please, Captain." She glowered in continuous expectation.

His laugh was truly nervous this time, as he produced another coin from behind her right ear and placed it within the woman's grasp. At that moment Captain Mephisto's magical powers performed a true miracle, and those that saw it rubbed their eyes in disbelief. Mrs. Murphy actually smiled.

"Thank you, Captain," she chirped, "and I hope you have a pleasant evening and a good show." She then disappeared into the boardinghouse.

The captain sighed as he latched his suitcase, and then continued down the stairs. He turned left and headed in the direction of the theater by way of the alley.

The raven landed on Eddie's shoulder as the boy pretended to lean disinterestedly against a lamppost across the street.

"Well," said Eddie, "so much for secret devils or trained animals hidden in the suitcase. It was practically empty."

"Maybe his demon is invisible like yours," the raven suggested. "Why, it could be enjoying the evening air from its master's shoulder right at this very moment."

"Ya mean just like you, ya *freeloader*?" McCobber sneered. "Besides, invisible or not, I could see any demon who was out in the open," he said proudly. "It's me second sight, ya know."

"Ah, second sight," said the raven. "Does that mean that by the second time you look at something, you have usually imagined it is something else entirely?"

"Don't twist my words," McCobber threatened, "but speaking of being invisible, since you are not, maybe you should find a less conspicuous place to rest that mangy black carcass of yours."

"I'm afraid he's right, Raven," Eddie said apologetically. "You do rather draw attention to yourself."

"Oh, all right," the raven conceded. "I'll see you boys in the alley by the stage door." And with a few strong wing beats, the bird flew effortlessly up and over the rooftops.

"Aaach," whispered McCobber, watching the raven bank and glide from view. "If you ask me, that feathered scoundrel could have easily carried off a pillowcase filled with one measly cat and a skinny old rooster!"

"Shhh," Eddie whispered as he crossed the street and turned down the alley. "We had better keep an

eye on the real suspect before he gives us the slip."

There was a little alley that cut between the boardinghouse yard and the neighbor's yard. This dirt path met a larger alley that ran behind Mrs. Murphy's, the Allans', and the judge's houses. Where the two wagon-rutted pathways met, they formed a T intersection. When Eddie reached that point, he was surprised to find no one in sight in any direction. Puzzled, he stood in the center of the intersection,

wondering where the man could have vanished to in such a short time.

As he peered off in the direction of the theater, Eddie was startled when suddenly a dark figure appeared behind him. In a moment Mephisto had swept by him and on down the alleyway.

Eddie quickly pretended to walk in the opposite direction, paused behind a tree, and then proceeded to follow his quarry.

For the five or six blocks that was the length of the journey to the theater's alley, nothing of note happened. Soon Eddie and McCobber were watching from behind an old wooden barrel as Mephisto gave the stage door a series of three short raps. A moment later the door opened and the captain disappeared within.

The raven landed on the barrel's rim as Eddie knelt behind it. "That's weird," the bird said. "I wonder what our friend the captain was doing in Murphy's shed."

"So that's where he went," said Eddie.

"Maybe he had to take a leak," McCobber suggested.

"We'd better keep an eye on this guy," Eddie said. "He's up to something."

He then walked to the stage door and tried to open it. "Locked," he whispered. "I sure would like to see what goes on backstage with old Mephisto." He began to turn away, and then remembered something. "You know," he said, "I used to know somebody who worked here. . . ." He gingerly rapped three times himself.

"I'm comin'," a voice called from inside. The door opened, and an older black man in shirtsleeves and waistcoat appeared. "May I help you?"

Eddie was relieved at the sight of him. "Hello, Mr. Othello. Remember me?"

The man squinted, and tilted his head first to the left and then to the right. Then a smile slowly brightened his eyes. "Young Master Poe? Is that you?" he grinned. "Is that Eddie Poe?" Eddie smiled and nodded.

"Why, I'd hardly recognize you," he said, and laughed. "You're so grown. Look at you!" He shook his head. "But you still got your mother's eyes." The man patted the boy on the shoulder. "Now, what brings you down here on such a fine evening? You got a hankerin' to see a show?"

Eddie's smile broadened, and he was about to answer when—

"By golly!" said the old man with a sudden start. "You know, there's someone here who'd like to see you. Just hold on now, hold on!" He turned, peering into the dark passageway behind him. "Cap'n," he called. "Excuse me, Cap'n Mephisto?"

Eddie felt a wave of panic when he heard the name. "Ah, n-no. That's all right," he stammered. "You don't have to . . ."

As the man in front of him turned, Eddie got a glimpse into the hallway. There, not thirty feet away, stood his suspect conversing with a clown. For one flashing instant Eddie considered trying to duck and hide, but it was too late. The magician had looked their way, excused himself from his conversation, and begun retracing his steps back to the stage door.

"Beggin' your pardon, Cap'n," said Mr. Othello, beaming, "but I was pretty sure you'd like to say hello to this young gentleman. Cap'n Mephisto, meet Master Edgar Poe."

Mephisto looked at the older man in disbelief for a moment, and then steadied his gaze directly on Eddie. "Not Eliza's boy?" His intense stare flickered into a smile. "My Lord, so it is . . . so it is!" He shook the boy's hand warmly.

"Captain Mephisto here organized a benefit performance by the other players to raise money for your poor mother, just before the end there." Othello smiled sadly.

"Too little, too late, I am afraid," said the magician. "We all admired your mother so. She was such a lovely woman and a talented actress."

Eddie tried to speak but couldn't find the words.

"And how is that little sister of yours?" Mephisto continued. "She was so very little when . . . when . . ."

"Oh, Rosalie." Eddie finally found his voice again.

"She's fine, sir. I see her quite regularly. She lives with the McKenzies now, and they're friends with my foster parents, John and Fannie Allan."

"Ah, yes." He smiled. "I do remember now. My, they certainly have done well by you. Why, you're growing like a weed!"

"Hey, Mephisto!" called a loud, harsh voice from within the theater. "There you are. I want a word with you." A large, gruff man with a cigar in his mouth shoved his way into their midst.

"Listen, Mephisto," he continued, seemingly unaware of the others. "I wanted to talk to you about your act. It could use a little spicin' up. You know, more pizzazz. Like I told ya the other day, if you want to stay on the bill in this theater, you gotta keep up with the times."

"Why, uh, yes, Mr. Wood," said the captain, somewhat flustered. "I'll definitely take that into consideration."

"So what's all this?" The man's attention had shifted to Eddie. "If this kid's lookin' for a job, we don't have any. If he wants to see the show, it's two bits out front, just like all the rest of the yokels!"

"Excuse me, sir," said Othello politely, "but this is young Edgar Poe." He smiled. "He's the son of

the actors Elizabeth
and David Poe."

"Oooh, yeah. I remember."
He eyed Eddie as he took the
wet chewed cigar from between his
teeth and pointed at him with grubby wet
fingers. "Your old man never could hold
his liquor, could he?" He grinned a
greasy, snide grin.

Eddie felt himself go crimson
with rage. "Sir!" He was about to
unleash an unbridled assault of
verbal fury when the captain spoke.

"I beg your pardon, sir," he said
in a stern voice, "but I believe you
had better watch your tongue. The
Poes were friends of mine."

"Psssh!" The theater manager
turned on him with contempt. "That
figures! Maybe I've been too nice to you
for too long, old-timer," he sneered. "Maybe
I ought to drop your billing and your pay as of
tonight . . . as of *right now!*"

"Now, see here, Wood!" Mephisto started.

"Ah, keep it to yourself, Cappy!" Wood waved him

off. "I'm too busy to
mess with you now. We'll
handle this after the show!" He
turned away from Mephisto and stuck
his finger on the boy's chest. "And you."
He spat, then squinted. "Beat it!"

Eddie felt the big flat hand push him hard. The unexpected shove caught him off guard, and he lost his balance. He toppled backward. There was a bone-jarring smack as he hit the broken pavement of the alley. His palms burned from an attempt to break his fall. From the ground he saw Mr. Othello's apologetic face just before the stage door slammed shut.

Eddie was on his feet immediately, dusting himself off and cursing under his breath.

"Why that big oaf!" McCobber raged. "I say we go back in there and teach that cretin a lesson!"

"Yeah?" Eddie muttered. "You and what army?" He stormed over to the barrel where they had left the raven, and he kicked the slats. The bird jumped, then fluttered back onto the rim.

"Easy, boy. What happened?"

Eddie flopped back against the brick wall and slid down until he was seated on the ground. "Why is the world ruled by subhuman clods and vulgarians?" he said, fuming.

"I guess they wouldn't let you go backstage, eh?" the raven asked.

"It was a sneak attack!" McCobber growled. "Just give me a few minutes with that moron, and I'll wipe that smirk off his face!"

"So, what now?" The raven ignored the ranting little demon.

Eddie explained that not only had the theater manager made an affront to his parents, but he had also threatened to fire the magician. And even if Mephisto were somehow involved in this cat and rooster incident, there was no way Eddie was going to expose him now. The man had gone out of his way

to try to help his family before his mother died.

"I see," the raven said. Then, after a few moments of thoughtful silence, he added, "So, do you have two bits?"

Eddie looked up, confused—and McCobber looked up, annoyed. "What?" McCobber snapped.

"If Eddie's got two bits," the raven replied, "he should take in the show." Directing his comments to the boy, he said, "What have you got to lose? And it might take your mind off . . . well, you know . . . your troubles."

"TROUBLES?!" McCobber cried. "Don't be cute! And don't try to sugarcoat this! How's this kid supposed to forget that tomorrow he is doomed to be beaten within an inch of his life? TROUBLES!"

"All right, McCobber, knock it off!" Eddie said. He leaned his elbows onto his knees and ran his hands through his hair. "Yeah," he sighed, "maybe you're right, Raven. Since the prime suspect is beyond

reproach, I guess I might as well face the inevitable and get used to the idea that I am the scapegoat. In which case, dear Raven, your suggestion is a grand one. Why *not* spend my last night enjoying at least a bit of pleasure!" He stood up and dug deep into his pocket. A moment later he flipped a quarter into the air.

"McCobber, old friend," he said, smiling, "please allow me to treat you to this, our farewell fling. And you, our ebony companion." Eddie bowed slightly to the raven. "I am sorry that you cannot join us for this particular amusement, but we would be honored by the pleasure of your company for the journey home. Will you be here after the final curtain falls?"

"Then and evermore." He, too, bowed slightly and smiled.

"Ha ha ha . . . very funny!" snarled McCobber. "We'll see who's making with the gallows humor tomorrow morning!"

"Ah, but tomorrow, my dear McCobber," Eddie comforted. "Tomorrow is an eternity away, and tonight . . . Well, tonight stretches before us like a magic carpet!"

"Bah!" the imp grumbled. "You'll be lucky if that butcher Allan doesn't roll you into a carpet and dump you in an alley after he's taken his cat-o'-nine-tails to you."

"Tsk, tsk, McCobber." Eddie shook his head. "I did so hope you would get more into the spirit of the thing. Perhaps you just need a little time to yourself." And before the imp knew what hit him, Eddie had plucked McCobber from his shoulder and thrust him into the pocket of his frock coat. "You will just have to sit in there until you decide to be civil." Then, nodding slightly to the raven, Eddie lifted his chin, puffed out his chest, and with the air of an experienced man about town, strode down the alley toward the front of the theater.

"Enjoy the show," the raven called.

"We shall," Eddie called over his shoulder as he patted his pocket. "We shall!"

CHAPTER NINE

At the playhouse entrance a poster proclaimed the wonders of the show within. The theater offered a wide range of entertainments throughout the season, from the plays of Shakespeare to dramatic readings and lectures. This week featured a variety show in which an assortment of different acts would perform their particular specialties during the course of an evening. There was to be a pig act, dancers, jugglers, and then the main act: Captain Mephisto. It was his image featured on the poster.

"So what do you think, McCobber," Eddie whispered to the imp. "Could that demon we saw in the window last night be the true magic behind the magician?"

THE MYSTIFYING
CAPTAIN MEPHISTO
Will Astonish and Amaze!!

With His Fabulous

FABRIC of the PHARAOHS

★ ★ ★   Also Appearing   ★ ★ ★

MAYNARD AND HIS MAGNIFICENT PIG

THE GOLDEN VOICE OF NELLIE BOLYN

DANCING SENSATIONS YANNI & NATASIA

The **JUGGLING GIANNI BOYS**

"Bah!" McCobber sneered, peeking out from under the pocket flap. "I don't know about making birds *magically appear*, but I know how he makes them *disappear*." McCobber made a loud, chomping sound and finished with a long, exaggerated gulp.

A balcony seat was all Eddie could afford, but it was enough. From the moment he stepped into the theater he was engulfed in a whirl of ghostly memories and mixed emotions. Vague impressions of countless theaters and backstage dressing rooms swirled into one vivid image. Bathed in soft lamplight, his mother sat before a mirror applying makeup for the evening's performance. Eyeliner and rouge enhanced her already lovely features to an unearthly beauty. All the while she softly rehearsed her lines and occasionally turned to smile or wink at her two young sons.

The boys played near her in the crowded dressing room. Theirs was a world of fantasy amidst the satin and velvet costumes and well-worn props that flowed from the actress's trunk.

Then there was the performance itself. Eddie and his brother, Henry, loved to watch from the wings as she played her part,

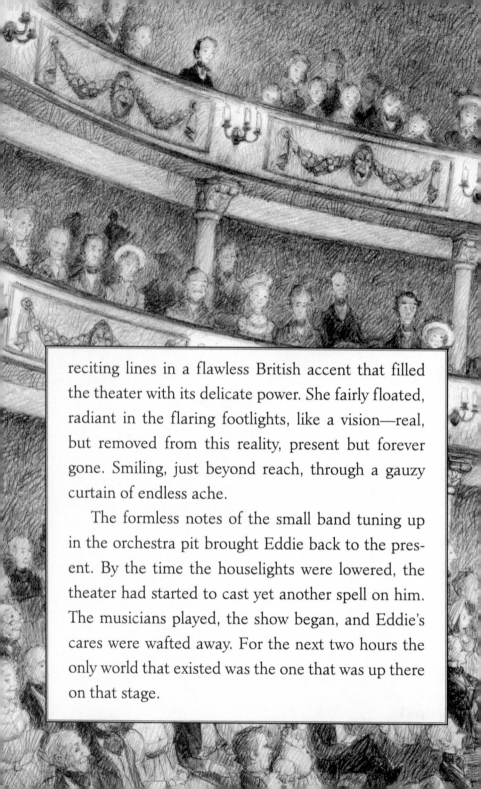

reciting lines in a flawless British accent that filled the theater with its delicate power. She fairly floated, radiant in the flaring footlights, like a vision—real, but removed from this reality, present but forever gone. Smiling, just beyond reach, through a gauzy curtain of endless ache.

The formless notes of the small band tuning up in the orchestra pit brought Eddie back to the present. By the time the houselights were lowered, the theater had started to cast yet another spell on him. The musicians played, the show began, and Eddie's cares were wafted away. For the next two hours the only world that existed was the one that was up there on that stage.

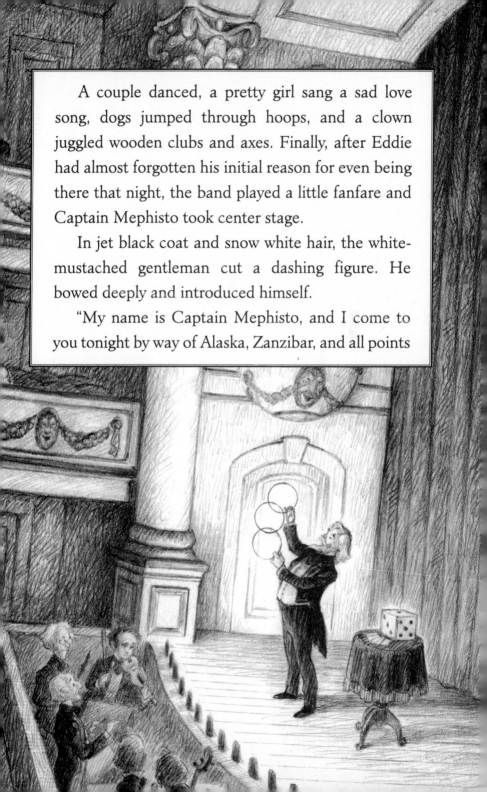

A couple danced, a pretty girl sang a sad love song, dogs jumped through hoops, and a clown juggled wooden clubs and axes. Finally, after Eddie had almost forgotten his initial reason for even being there that night, the band played a little fanfare and Captain Mephisto took center stage.

In jet black coat and snow white hair, the white-mustached gentleman cut a dashing figure. He bowed deeply and introduced himself.

"My name is Captain Mephisto, and I come to you tonight by way of Alaska, Zanzibar, and all points in between. It will be my distinct pleasure to share with you some of the rare wonders that I have collected on my far-flung voyages across the globe. Here, for example, I hold three simple rings forged by a Chinese silversmith in the seventh century." Holding the rings before the crowd, he proceeded to tangle, untangle, juggle, and manipulate the silvery hoops in mystifying ways. This was followed by delightful card tricks, sleight of hand, and all manner of conjuring.

Finally he told the fantastic story of how he and his crew had saved the life of a shipwrecked old man they'd found clinging to a chest in the middle of the Mediterranean Sea. It was only later that they learned that this ancient mariner was one of the most learned sorcerers of the mysterious Orient. By way of thanking Mephisto for saving his life, the sage gave the captain a priceless treasure.

An assistant then entered the stage carrying a jeweled coffer no bigger than a shoe box. Its lid and sides glistened in the footlights as it was carefully placed upon the table in front of the magician. Bowing deeply, the assistant then made his solemn exit.

"Within this beautiful box lies that old wizard's most cherished possession. The thing that he valued more than all the other wondrous objects he had ever owned. No, my friends, not silver or gold, not rubies, diamonds, or sapphires—for those are mere trinkets compared to this." Opening the box, he carefully withdrew a single piece of folded cloth. Then, as if handling a holy relic, he reverently unfolded it.

"And even though it was woven nearly two thousand years ago, it still retains its suppleness and strength." He ran it lovingly over the back of his hand and through his fingertips; caressing it gently, he displayed its silken thinness.

"But within its delicate folds, deep magic dwells, for this deceptively simple fabric is enchanted." Grasping it between his fingertips, he held it out full length before him, where it hung, curtainlike.

"For it giveth . . ." With a graceful gesture he pulled the cloth to one side, revealing the jeweled box that had been momentarily curtained beneath it. He lifted the lid. Glistening inside was a pile of golden coins. He grabbed a handful and let them clink one by one back into the nearly overflowing chest.

Holding the cloth up as before, he added, "And it taketh away!" Once more he whisked the fabric aside, revealing that this time the box, coins and all, had vanished.

"Wow. How does he do that?" Eddie whispered. "His hands were in plain sight the whole time!"

"Yeah," McCobber marveled. "His demon must have some physique. Even I couldn't tote cargo like that gold around. Must be all the raw meat that thing eats."

"But," continued the magician, "as I said before, this cloth holds its magic deep within the weave of its enchanted threads." He gestured with the cloth, making it appear to dance a graceful ballet. Then, running it through his fingers, he added, "Only those who know its secrets can share in its bountiful gifts." He gently plucked from its folds first one gold coin and then another, until a small pile had grown on the table.

"And yet, one can grow weary harvesting even the loveliest of fruits one at a time. I have learned that a bit of a twist can speed things up considerably." Then, as he wrung the cloth between his hands, coins began to rain from it onto the table.

The audience oohed and applauded. "So how do I get a demon like that?" Eddie asked.

"There you go." McCobber huffed. "Imaginin' that the grass is always greener. But be careful what you wish for, laddie. Your soul is a mighty high price to pay for a rag that spits gold."

"Ah, ladies and gentlemen," continued Mephisto, acknowledging the applause. "Don't be fooled. As King Midas learned centuries ago, man cannot live by gold alone."

"See," agreed McCobber.

"And," said the captain, "a truly wondrous miracle is one that can supply its owner with *all* his needs." Taking a medium-size cloth bag from his pocket, he deposited the coins one by one into it.

"Gold is good," he went on, "but very hard to digest." He placed the bag of coins in the center of the table.

"There are times when the sight of a well-prepared meal, for example, can be more welcome than a king's ransom." Once again he lifted the cloth and curtained the tabletop from view. "Times," he continued, "when a stuffed foul or a plump rabbit ready for dinner are worth more than their weight in gold." Lowering the cloth revealed no apparent change in the bag. It lay on the table as before.

Mephisto gave an embarrassed laugh and cleared his throat. "Did I mention that this wonderful fabric originated in the far-off land of an ancient kingdom, where the English language was never uttered? Communication can be a problem even in the realm of miracles." Looking into the bag, he grimaced, then turned to the audience in dismay.

"As you see, intention and understanding

do not always coincide." He pulled out a white rabbit and a fluttering dove. Both were wearing white
starched collars with matching black vests and ties.
"These handsome fellows are indeed ready to have
dinner. Unfortunately, I was hoping that they would
be dinner." The audience laughed.

"Hmmm," whispered Eddie. "Two animals hidden
in a cloth bag. Does this look familiar?"

"You know," McCobber said, and laughed,
"maybe I have seen this trick somewhere before, now
that you mention it!"

"Like in our own backyard, perhaps?" said Eddie.

"If you will allow me," continued Mephisto, "I
would like to try that again." He gently returned the
animals to the bag and placed it back in
the center of the table. Then, holding
the cloth up again, he said, "*Ing-ah-
lah, Ting-ah-lah, Tock-ah-fer. Ing-ah-lah,
Fing-ah-lah, Foo!*"

When he lowered the cloth,
the bag on the table seemed
little changed. "Hmmm.
Perhaps I need to

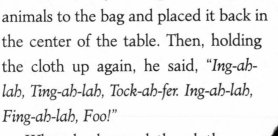

review my ancient grammar."

Lifting the bag, he peered into it.

"Well, at least now we seem to be on the right track." From it he pulled first a silver spoon, then a knife, a fork, a crystal goblet, and a porcelain plate. He then arranged them on the table like a place setting. With a flourish he snapped the bag in the air, turning it into a freshly ironed napkin, which he promptly tucked into his collar. "You see." He smiled. "A little perseverance can pay off."

Holding the cloth up again, he said loudly, "CHOW TIME!" Mephisto swept the cloth away to reveal a roast bird of golden brown, resting on a green bed of parsley.

"Ah, yes!" he exclaimed. "And now the final touch. A fine wine, an 1815 chardonnay, perhaps . . ." Holding the magic cloth in his hands like a bottle, he proceeded to pour a deep, red liquid from it into the glass.

"I had hoped for a white wine, but . . ." He lifted the glass and sipped. "Ah, an 1814 burgundy. Still a fine choice."

"Now if you'll excuse me," he said, picking up knife and fork. "I did miss my lunch today, and *this*

is still hot." Mephisto began to carve the roast bird, and as he did so he mused, "I do wonder whatever became of our friend the rabbit."

Suddenly he stopped, looked at the bird, and then

out at the audience. "Unfortunately," he said, pulling open the bird and peering into it, "this still looks a little rare!"

Reaching in, he withdrew the flapping dove and nose-twitching rabbit. "Well," he laughed. " I guess I did say 'stuffed,' after all, didn't I?"

Holding up the rabbit and dove, he stepped out from behind the table and bowed to the applauding crowd. The band played and the curtain came down.

As the houselights came up and the audience started to leave, Eddie sat deep in thought.

"So now what do I do?" he asked.

"Why, I'd go tell that old gob you know what his demon does on its night off." McCobber fumed. "And if he doesn't fess up and take the blame, you'll expose him!"

"And just how do you propose I do that?" Eddie asked. "'Excuse me, Captain Mephisto, but my demon thinks your demon should apologize'?"

"Well, why not?" asked McCobber. "If the little devil can dish it out, he's also got to learn to take it."

Eddie didn't answer, but sat pondering as the theater emptied and the lights dimmed.

CHAPTER TEN

Well?"

Eddie finally emerged from his thoughts, realizing that he wasn't sure just how long he had been sitting in the dark, quiet theater.

"Well?" asked McCobber again impatiently. "Are we going to sit here all night, or what?"

"I'm going backstage to tell him I liked the show," Eddie said.

"And then . . . ," said McCobber.

"And that's it," Eddie answered. "He was a friend of my family and offered help to my dying mother. If it was his demon that stuck our cat and that rooster into a bag, well, that's just a secret I'll have to keep, that's all!"

"It's your hide, but if you ask me—"

"I didn't ask you," Eddie snapped as he headed up the aisle toward the back of the theater. "Now, are you coming or not?"

"Very funny," McCobber said. "Like I've really got a choice."

The place appeared to be empty, which was a relief. The last thing Eddie wanted was to have another run-in with that manager. The place was so empty, in fact, that he was beginning to wonder if he might have missed the magician as well.

Slipping into the wings, he heard voices
being raised backstage. Eddie ducked behind
a section of scenery. It was Mephisto and the
manager, and they appeared to be having an
argument.

"If you want to fire me, that's one thing,"
Mephisto said, "but at least pay me what
you owe me!"

"Come on, old-timer," the manager
sneered. "Just tell me how you do
some of that stuff, and you'll get
your dough."

Mephisto became indignant. "You, sir, have no right to ask that of me. Those are trade secrets."

"All right, all right," said the manager, trying a different angle. "Listen, I happen to know this young magician who's got real style—you know, lots of pizzazz!—but he needs a gimmick. Now, with your tricks and his pizzazz, that guy could really go places!"

"Well," said Mephisto, "he will have to figure out his own 'gimmick'. I am still using *mine*."

"Look, he's willing to pay," the manager coaxed. "I could even cut you in . . . maybe split it fifty-fifty?"

"You are asking me to sell my secrets for a few paltry dollars?" Mephisto said. "This is my act, my livelihood. Thank you, but NO!" He turned to go.

"Listen, Cappy, you're not quite gettin' any younger," said the manager, roughly grabbing the older gentleman's shoulder, "and you sure can't take it with you!"

"I am warning you, sir." The captain spoke with growing impatience. "You had better unhand me."

"I am through being nice!" The manager grabbed

Mephisto by both shoulders and forcibly turned him. "TELL ME NOW!"

Eddie's growing rage drew him from the shadows.

"I am warning you . . . ," Mephisto said, angrily facing his assailant.

"So where are these secrets?" the manager asked scornfully. "Under that goofy hat?" With a powerful swing he knocked the hat from the magician's head, then quickly grabbed the front of his vest. "Or are they in here?"

Suddenly there was a muffled scream that seemed to come from Mephisto's chest. A pair of small hands burst from his vest pockets, grabbing the manager's wrists in a viselike grip. A dove appeared in an explosion of flapping wings, buffeting the now shrieking man's face.

"I warned you!" Mephisto cried. Eddie froze, terrified.

The small hands tightened their grip even more, as the manager sunk to his knees, crying, "STOP! STOP!" In an instant the little fingers were at Mr. Wood's throat, choking him. Eyes bulging, the man gasped and gagged.

"NO! NO!" Mephisto cried as he grabbed the little arms, trying to wrench them from the man's throat. "Release him. . . . REE . . . LEASE . . . HIM!" Finally the magician pried the clutching hands free, and the manager fell backward, nearly senseless.

"Run!" Mephisto shouted to the manager. "Run! You have angered it, and I am no longer in control. Run!"

Hands to his throat, gasping for breath, the terrified manager got to his feet. Knocking Eddie out of the way, he ran past the scenery flats and into the dark passage. Running feet echoed down

the hallway as he hit the door to the outside with a bang. It slammed shut, and then nothing. . . . Silence.

A shiver ran through Eddie when he realized that they were now completely alone.

He heard Mephisto inhale deeply. Then the magician threw back his head, and an explosion of maniacal laughter split the air.

"Ha, ha, ha! Well done, Dante. Well done!"

As the man cackled, the small demonic arms flailed victoriously from his chest, seeming to glory in its master's joy.

As Mephisto's laughter finally subsided, his gaze fell on Eddie.

"Well." He sighed heavily. "I guess you know our secret."

"Oh no," McCobber whispered.

Eddie began to back away slowly. "I won't tell anyone. I promise."

Mephisto took a step closer. "Don't be afraid." The little arms reached out blindly toward the boy. "We won't hurt *you*."

Eddie took another step backward, only to find himself trapped by the framework of a scenery flat and its support.

Mephisto inched forward, smiling. "Dante just wants to be friends."

The old man had taken another step closer, when suddenly his vest ripped open. A dark shape with flashing eyes and teeth lunged forth. McCobber screamed, and Eddie turned away, covering his face with his arm.

"Dante, you silly boy. That's no way to make friends." The old man chuckled softly, and Eddie lowered his arm.

Perched on Mephisto's shoulder was a playful monkey, ruffling the man's white hair.

Eddie released his breath with a loud sigh. "So that's your demon!"

Mephisto laughed. "My demon, my angel, my blessing, and my curse. Yes, that's Dante! But I would be lost without him." Just then the dove flew from the darkness and landed on a nearby backdrop. "Ah, yes, and I can't forget Gabriel, or"—he lifted the flap of his coat pocket, revealing the white rabbit's twitching nose—"Lepus. We are a team, you know."

"Pssht," McCobber muttered. "A monkey passin' himself off as a demon. Why, it's enough to make a self-respecting imp turn in his horns!"

CHAPTER ELEVEN

Eddie approached the old man and monkey with caution. Too much had happened in the last few minutes for him to be completely at his ease.

"Go ahead," Mephisto reassured him. "He's calmed down now. Most of that was for dramatic effect anyway. He loves to put on a show."

The boy reached out slowly, and Dante, with surprising gentleness, took him by the finger and shook it.

"There, you see." Mephisto smiled. "You have shaken hands and are now friends for life." Eddie laughed.

"I am sorry you had to see all that," Mephisto apologized. "But once a performer reaches a certain age, you start to lose your edge, and then every roughneck in the business is ready to throw you out as a has-been."

"That guy was a real creep," said Eddie. "I was glad you and Dante scared the devil out of him. Besides, the audience loved your act."

Mephisto smiled sadly. "Thank you, Edgar. But times have changed. Once, we played only the largest theaters to sold-out crowds." He stroked the monkey as it began reaching over to preen Eddie's hair.

"Well, one thing's for sure," said Mephisto. "Dante certainly has taken a shine to you. I believe he would like to sit on your shoulder. Do you mind?"

McCobber hissed in Eddie's ear. "He wouldn't dare!"

"Sure!" And as the boy moved his shoulder closer, the monkey climbed aboard.

McCobber fumed. "Aaach, you filthy beast! Just make sure you stay on your own side and don't be throwin' any of that monkey feces in this direction!"

Mephisto handed Eddie a nut. "Here, give him this. It's long past his dinnertime. He's been stuck in the harness much longer than normal today."

The little hands took the morsel, and then Eddie
watched Dante cup them to his face and greedily devour the nut. "So," said Eddie, looking toward
the straps and cagelike structure that showed from
beneath the unbuttoned vest. "So it was really Dante
hiding under there and performing all those tricks?"

"Well," Mephisto said, pulling another nut from his pocket. "He's really only working during the Enchanted Cloth bit, but he does have to stay hidden for the whole act. Would you like to see how it works?"

"Oh . . . Ah . . ." Eddie suddenly felt exposed himself. "I . . . I live in the neighborhood and just happened to be passing by when you came out this evening."

"Ah, I see," Mephisto continued. "So, you saw her stop me for the rent?"

Eddie nodded. "And it didn't look like Dante could have been in the trunk then. It was practically empty."

"Ah, yes." Mephisto smiled slyly. "I knew that if we encountered our dear landlady she would be expecting the rent. And just to put to rest any suspicions she might have had about me harboring pets, I took the precaution of putting the money in the suitcase and the monkey under my vest."

"Then he must have been already tired of hiding under there by the time you got to the theater," Eddie said.

"Actually," said Mephisto, "I took an opportunity to put him in the suitcase once I knew we were in the clear."

"That's why you went into the shed!" Eddie exclaimed, before he realized what he was doing.

Mephisto stopped short. "How did you . . . ?" Then his eyes widened, as he finally understood. "Oh, my

goodness. You are the boy who was out in the yard this morning, aren't you?"

Eddie nodded and looked down.

"Oh, my boy," Mephisto cried. "I am so sorry that the blame fell on you. When I heard the commotion this morning and looked out to see them release the rooster and cat from that bag, I suspected Dante was somehow involved."

"Suspected?" Eddie asked. "Didn't you know?"

"I was confused." Mephisto suddenly looked helpless and old. "I must have been asleep when he escaped. You see, we had been up late going over and over a new routine. When we finally went to bed, it must have been well past one a.m. I went out like a light, but Dante must have been restless. And when that infernal rooster crowed at sunup, like it always does, he must have taken matters into his own hands, so to speak."

"He probably heard our cat yowling too," Eddie added. "I was just getting to sleep myself when Cairo started in. I can't really blame Dante, though. When I finally did get to sleep, I dreamt that I had silenced them. In fact, I was still dreaming when I woke up and found myself out on the lawn."

"So that's why they blamed you," Mephisto said. "You had sleepwalked into the wrong place at the wrong time."

Eddie shrugged. "I guess Dante really does know magic after all. He made everyone believe that I'd performed that miraculous act."

"But one thing puzzled me this morning," said Mephisto thoughtfully, "and it puzzles me still. Where did he get the bag? It wasn't one of mine."

"That was my pillowcase," Eddie explained. "I was trying to make Cairo be quiet last night when I . . . ah . . . sort of 'accidentally' threw my pillow out the window." He smiled sheepishly, half-embarrassed. "I found it in the yard this morning without its case. I can remember yanking on some fabric in my dream, so sometime while I was sleepwalking I must have pulled the pillowcase off the pillow. I guess it was still in my hand when I walked over to the judge's. And

Cairo—well, he's pretty curious, so he probably just came over to see what I was doing in the chicken yard."

"Aha," said Mephisto, fitting the pieces together. "So Dante, who apparently arrived at the same time you did, saw a familiar prop—the cloth bag—and two animals he wanted to make disappear—the cat and the rooster. Then, just as he had been trained to do, he stuffed them into the bag and hoped they would vanish!"

"Or turn into dinner," Eddie said, and laughed.

"He did improvise a dramatic touch that's not in the act, however," said Mephisto, "by hanging the bag from the weather vane."

"Maybe," Eddie added, "once they *didn't* disappear but actually became noisier . . . Maybe he panicked and tried to ditch the evidence."

"And ended up framing the neighbor kid," Mephisto said, as they both burst into relieved laughter.

As the laughter subsided, Mephisto became serious again. "I am sorry I was too much of a coward to stand up and take the blame, but I was afraid . . . afraid that if Mrs. Murphy found out about my teammates, we would find ourselves on the street. And frankly, I was terrified that I might have to expose the secret of my act." He hung his head, ashamed.

"It's all right," Eddie said. "I understand."

"But you were probably punished," Mephisto said, raising his head.

"Not yet," said Eddie. "But don't worry. Whatever it is, it will be nothing compared to you losing the roof over your head and damaging your career."

"Thank you, Edgar," said Mephisto, "but as things have turned out, I won't be needing the room beyond tonight anyway. I'm catching the five o'clock stagecoach tomorrow morning. So, perhaps if I spoke to the judge and Mr. Allan, we could get this all cleared up."

"Please, Captain," Eddie said. "You needn't worry."

"Perhaps if I had some money that you could give to the judge," the magician continued, "then maybe he could buy a new rooster. Unfortunately, I'm a little short right now, what with just paying the rent and not getting paid for this engagement. But I could send something once I reach my next booking."

"Captain," Eddie said with resolve, "I am the one

who owes you. You befriended my dying mother years ago by helping to pay my family's debts. Please let me handle this minor situation."

Mephisto smiled. "Edgar, your mother would be very proud of you." Then he opened the suitcase, and Dante climbed inside. "Are you sure there is nothing I can do?"

Eddie smiled. "There is one thing, sir. Would you give me the honor of allowing me to walk the Great Captain Mephisto to his boardinghouse?"

"Young man," Mephisto said proudly, "the honor would be all mine."

CHAPTER TWELVE

Just as Eddie and Mephisto were about to leave the theater, the captain thought he may have forgotten something. "You go ahead, my boy. I'll meet you outside in a minute."

The moment Eddie stepped out of the stage door, the raven flew to him. Breathless with anticipation, he had waited through the entire evening and had grown more and more restless as first the theater-goers and then the actors had left the building. When finally the manager had burst out of the same door, running for his life, the poor bird had been beside himself with worry.

"Where the devil—" he blurted, landing on Eddie's shoulder. Then he immediately stopped talking, upon hearing Mephisto open the door behind them.

"I must be getting old. I was sure I'd left my boardinghouse key in the dressing room, but there it was in my pocket. Well!" He smiled, a bit surprised to see a large black bird peering at him from Eddie's shoulder. "You didn't tell me you had a friend of your own. What a beautiful bird! It is yours, I take it?"

"Oh, yes," Eddie said proudly. "He is my friend, but I can't say I think of him as belonging to me necessarily. He pretty much comes and goes as he pleases."

The raven cawed, and Eddie scratched the bird's head. "Sorry, old friend. I nearly forgot that I had left you out here." The bird closed his eyes and lowered his head in rapture. "Everything is all right now," Eddie said softly.

"Are you going to introduce me?" Mephisto asked, smiling.

"Forgive me," Eddie said. "I must be forgetting my manners. Raven, I would like you to meet my new friend, Captain Mephisto. Captain Mephisto, this is Raven."

"Pleased to make your acquaintance, friend Raven." Mephisto reached out to touch the bird's head. Raven cocked his head, eying the man suspiciously.

"Sorry," Eddie apologized. "It sometimes takes a little while with him."

"Perfectly understandable," Mephisto said. "One can never be too careful these days."

Eddie offered to carry the suitcase as they walked the dark, quiet streets back toward the boardinghouse and his home. Mephisto reminisced about happier

times, when the Poes had been a young married couple and they'd had all the world before them. Eddie felt as though he had discovered a long lost uncle who had truly known and understood his parents.

The boy openly showed his excitement at hearing these remembrances, and hung on every word. Listening to Mephisto's stories made these shadowy figures from his past more solid—more real.

Just as the man was finishing a tale, and the boy was laughing, the raven flew from one to the other. Landing on Mephisto's shoulder, the raven lowered his head as if to say, *You may scratch me now.*

"Well," said Mephisto, "what's this?"

"It appears," Eddie said, "that you have made yet another friend tonight."

"My dear Edgar." Mephisto spoke using his stage voice. "I have had the pleasure of traveling the world over and playing before the crowned heads of Europe, but never, no never, have I ever been more honored." He reached up and scratched the raven's head. The bird closed his eyes and purred a raven-y kind of purr.

"Oh, brother," McCobber grumbled.

As their footsteps fell on rutted streets and cobblestones, their conversation journeyed to ever broadening horizons: Mephisto's voyages and adventures, and Eddie's love of books and poetry.

"Edgar, I'd like to ask your opinion about something," Mephisto said as they turned onto their street. "You are obviously a person of discerning tastes, with more than his share of the theater in his blood, so yours is an opinion I would value."

"Yes, sir." Eddie felt pleased.

"It's about the act," Mephisto continued. "I'm always trying to improve it, and I wondered if you saw any way we could make it better."

"Well . . ." Eddie felt the pleasure of the honor take on the weight of responsibility. "Well, I know this is going to sound silly, but I somehow got it into my head that you had a real demon helping you out. That it wasn't the cloth that produced the magic but a demon hidden behind it."

"Yes." Mephisto was suddenly interested. "Go on."

"Well," Eddie continued, "that made it all seem less like a magician's trick, less like you were simply pulling coins out of a cloth. The notion that you were enlisting the help of a demon to produce those objects gave the act a slightly dangerous and otherworldly edge. And then, backstage, the image of those little hands bursting out of your chest. It was as if all my worst fears had come true, and the demon had gotten out of control. The horror of it was fantastic!"

"Yes," Mephisto laughed. "I know I'll never forget the effect Dante's appearance had at that moment. So you think having a demon helper is more mysterious than an enchanted cloth?"

"Maybe not more mysterious," Eddie said, "but creepier, for sure."

"I'll remember that," McCobber spat.

Mephisto was intrigued. "So you think that if I imply that there is a demon at work, and perhaps show hints of its existence, that might make for a better show?"

"Exactly!" Eddie said. "It was the idea that it was hidden. Something we weren't supposed to see. Something frightening. And then to hear that scream and see those grasping hands—it sent my senses reeling. But the moment I knew it was really a monkey, the excitement was over. What had been unbelievably horrifying was suddenly funny."

"Yes, that is always the challenge," the magician said, "to show just enough to excite the imagination, yet not enough to expose the trick. Ah, but *how* is the big question."

"What if Dante wore a disguise?" Eddie asked. "Something like a costume or makeup, so that from the audience, even if they caught a glimpse of him, he would appear to be a devil or a demon?"

"Hmmm," Mephisto replied. "Maybe that would work. . . . Perhaps a mask or horns, something like that?"

"Yes." That gave Eddie an idea. "You know, we have this old set of puppets up in our attic, and one of them is a devil. I bet with a little work it could be adapted into a costume for Dante. It's just about his size. You can have it, if you'd like."

"Why, thank you, Edgar," said Mephisto. "That does sound like the perfect thing. But I couldn't take part of someone's collection."

"My uncle Galt didn't want them anymore," Eddie said. "He told me if I didn't want them, he was going to throw them away. You might as well put that one to good use."

"Well, in that case . . . ," Mephisto said. They had reached the sidewalk in front of Murphy's boardinghouse.

"Great," said Eddie excitedly. "I'll just cut through the lots, sneak up the stairs, and be right back."

"Edgar, you know it's late," Mephisto whispered, "and you're probably going to be in trouble for staying out late as it is. Maybe this should wait."

"Aren't you leaving at five in the morning?" Eddie asked.

"Yes, but—"

"Well, I'd better do it now, then." Eddie started to go.

"What if I send Dante with you?" Mephisto suggested. "He could climb down using the tree in your backyard. That way you would only have to sneak in once. It might reduce the risk of you getting caught."

"Good idea," Eddie agreed.

They walked quietly to the back of Murphy's house and stood in the shadows. From there Eddie was within easy distance of his back door, and Mephisto would have a clear view of the attic window.

The magician asked Eddie to set the suitcase down, and within seconds the monkey was perched up on his shoulder. The raven cocked his head inquisitively. Mephisto pulled a cloth bag from his pocket and handed it to Eddie.

"Put the puppet in here," Mephisto said. "It will be easier for him to carry. And as for you, Mr. Dante." Mephisto addressed the monkey. "You listen to Edgar and come directly back here to me when he tells you to." The monkey looked thoughtful, then started picking his nose.

"Well," Mephisto said, extending his hand, "I guess we should say good-bye now. Edgar Poe, it has been my extreme pleasure to meet you, and your raven."

Eddie felt a twinge of loss as they warmly shook hands. He didn't know when, or if, their paths would ever cross again. He wouldn't have been able to imagine that he would meet someone who could, with such sincere affection, bring the memory of his parents so magically back to life. In this, if nothing else, the man who stood before him now was truly a worker of miracles.

"And we will *never* forget the Great Mephisto!" These were the only words Eddie could find. That is, until Dante interjected a typically simian "Ooh, ooh, ooh."

"Or his demon," Eddie added with a smile, and the two friends laughed.

As the monkey leapt onto Eddie's shoulder, the raven flew to a nearby tree. Before Eddie turned to go, a final nod of mutual friendship passed between the old gentleman and the boy. Within a few minutes Eddie had made it through the moonlight-spattered lawns and up to the back door. He eased open the squeaky screen door and was soon on his way up the back stairs.

By the time he opened the trapdoor to the attic, he was breathless. It was only then that he realized he had come up three flights of stairs without taking a single breath. Up here he could light a candle without worry, and he quickly did so. The puppet still hung from the rafters just where he had left it. The papier-mâché head was cracked up the back, and it separated easily from the empty cloth body.

Eddie placed the puppet's head on his own. "See,

Dante, you can wear this like a hat." He then gave it to the monkey.

Dante imitated Eddie, but because his head was much smaller than the boy's, the puppet's head completely covered his own. The monkey's face disappeared inside the papier-mâché devil's.

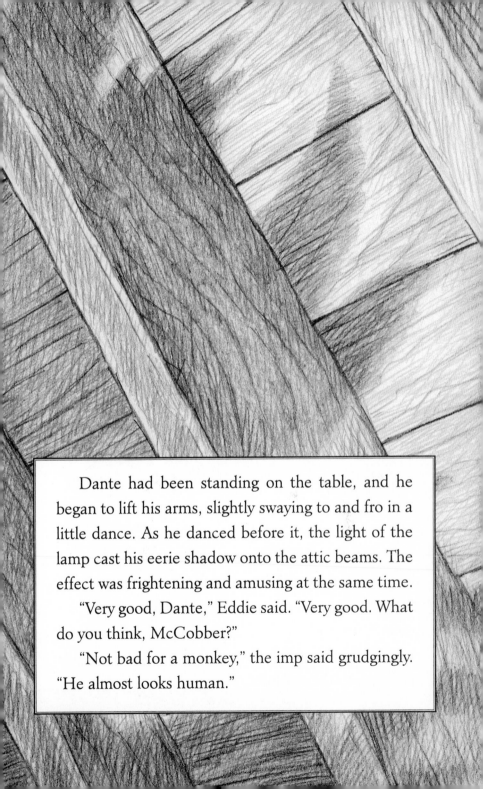

Dante had been standing on the table, and he began to lift his arms, slightly swaying to and fro in a little dance. As he danced before it, the light of the lamp cast his eerie shadow onto the attic beams. The effect was frightening and amusing at the same time.

"Very good, Dante," Eddie said. "Very good. What do you think, McCobber?"

"Not bad for a monkey," the imp said grudgingly. "He almost looks human."

"All right, Dante," Eddie said, removing the mask. "We'd better send you on your way." He opened the cloth sack Mephisto had given him, and paused. "This time it's my turn to fill the bag." He smiled as he placed the puppet's head and body within and drew the string. Then he placed the string over the monkey's head so the bag hung across his back like a little backpack. "Now you can use both hands to climb with."

Eddie opened the window. "Okay, Dante, take that back down there to Captain Mephisto." He pointed to the silhouette that waited across the yard. "And please don't get into any trouble."

The monkey started to climb out onto the sill, then suddenly turned around. Taking Eddie's finger in his hand, he gently shook it. The boy laughed.

"Well, look at the little goody-goody!" McCobber growled.

In an instant Dante had gone out the window, scampered to the edge of the roof, and leapt to a nearby tree limb. Moments later the dark figure on the lawn was joined by a smaller silhouette. Mephisto looked up and waved. Eddie waved back, and in another moment the man and monkey had disappeared into the shadows.

CHAPTER THIRTEEN

Eddie stood for a moment, wondering if everything that had happened during the last twenty-four hours was real, or McCobber-inspired. A loud flutter announced the raven's arrival on the windowsill.

"So that little devil's our demon, ay?" he asked.

"Now, don't go lettin' your imagination run away with you, Raven," McCobber said. "That thing only *wishes* it were a demon!"

"Well, he sure had us going." Eddie yawned. "I don't know about you two, but I'm ready to hit the hay."

They said their good-nights and Eddie stealthily made his way downstairs. Safe inside his room, he closed the door and by the light of the moon struck a match. As he lit the candle, he became aware of a presence in the room.

"So, you've finally come back, have you?" At the sound of John Allan's voice, Eddie nearly jumped out of his skin.

"JEEZ-LOWEEZ!" McCobber shouted into Eddie's ear.

"Good grief!" cried Eddie. "What are *you* doing here?"

"I assume you have a good explanation for being out all night!" Allan left the chair where he had been seated, and stepped into the light.

"Uh—I—" Eddie stammered. "I was carrying out my investigation."

"And . . ." Allan's stare bore down on him.

"And," Eddie answered, clearing his throat, "I am still innocent."

"And your proof?" Allan asked, unfazed.

"Nothing you would accept," Eddie answered with a note of pride in his voice.

"You're right," Allan replied with disdain. "Nothing I would accept." There was a long pause, and then, "I suppose you know what this means."

"Yes, sir." Eddie knew.

"We will deal with it in the morning." Allan turned to leave, then added, "Sleep well, Edgar."

"Good night, sir," Eddie replied.

"What a jerk," McCobber spat as Eddie changed into his nightshirt.

"It would have been nice to prove him wrong to his face," Eddie said, climbing into bed. "But tonight, somehow, what he thinks of me doesn't seem to matter that much." He leaned over and blew out the candle.

To his surprise, Eddie slept soundly that night; even his imagination and McCobber must have been tired, for not even a dream disturbed his slumber. Then, almost as if someone or something had poked him in the stomach, he was awake. It was still black outside, but there was something going on. A voice was calling to him from the yard.

As he opened the window, the voice filled the room. Eddie rubbed his eyes, wondering if he were dreaming, for there, near Judge Washington's poultry yard, stood a figure holding a lantern. At his feet rested a familiar suitcase.

"Could that be who I think it is?" Eddie wondered aloud.

"My name is Mephisto," the figure spoke, directing his voice to the surrounding houses. "I am a necromancer, and I am here to make amends!" Chickens clucked and fluttered as lamps were lit and windows were slid open. "You see before you a haunted man."

Eddie heard a window open and saw John Allan thrust his wondering head into the night. Moments later the judge leaned out his upstairs window, cursing. And across the lot the distinctive silhouette of Mrs. Murphy stood in her kitchen doorway.

"Yes," Mephisto continued, "haunted in more ways than one. For yesterday at this exact time and in this same place, an innocent party was blamed for my negligence. I speak of course of the cat and rooster incident and the boy who appeared to have performed the cruel prank. Well, I am here now to explain my involvement in this unfortunate matter and to once and for all clear his good name!"

Even in the darkness Eddie could feel the eyes of all assembled upon him, and he couldn't help but shrink away a bit from the window at which he stood.

"Throughout the years my studies of the magical arts have taken me to the farthest corners of the known world and into the realm of the unknown. I was privileged to be the student of an ancient mage who not only taught me all he knew, but also gave me a wonderful, and at times frightening, gift. He bequeathed to me a demon, or an imp, as it were. A small devil who was bound to me by certain oaths and incantations. Bound to be my servant and helper, and to travel with me in secret wherever I go." As he gestured to the suitcase at his feet, a low growl rose from within.

A gasp of realization issued from Mrs. Murphy, immediately followed by the cry of the boy who stood next to her in the boardinghouse kitchen. "I knew," he cried. "I just *knew* it!"

"Unfortunately," Mephisto continued, "it has on rare occasions managed to escape from my control and scamper about unchecked. Sadly, last night was just one of those occasions. For while I lay asleep, in a state of mental exhaustion, the demon managed to wriggle free of its magical bonds,

and in no time was up to its impish antics—right here, beneath your very windows."

Suddenly there was an even louder growl, and the suitcase began to bang and thump. All within earshot gasped. The magician turned quickly, putting his boot upon the case.

"STOP, DANTE! Instinimus nostrum!" The thumping slowly ceased, and the suitcase grew quiet.

"As you can see," Mephisto said, addressing his audience once again, "one must be always on one's guard with such creatures. Fortunately, he is primarily a prankster. Unfortunately, his fun is always at the expense of others.

"And so, in the wee hours of yesterday morning, when the demon heard the spine-tingling yowl of the cat and the eye-opening crow of the rooster, he saw a chance for deviltry. But before his fun could begin, he needed one more playmate to make the game complete: a scapegoat, a dupe, an unknowing innocent on whom the blame for the cruel joke would fall. Ah!" Mephisto's eyes widened in imitation of the mischievous imp as he rubbed his hands with relish. "How about the innocent neighbor lad? Using his psychic powers, the demon called the boy out of his bed and into this yard. Still clutching his own pillow, the boy walked in a sleeplike trance. How gleefully Dante must have stripped that pillow of its case. Then, using the boy himself as bait, the imp lured the trusting cat to within reach.

"In a lightning-quick move the demon snatched up the unsuspecting animal and tossed it into the empty pillowcase. Then, in a twinkling, the demon threw open the gate to the chicken yard and chased down the hapless rooster.

"It was at that moment that I, sensing great disturbances in the necromantic membranes of my magician's brain, finally roused myself from slumber. There, from my bedroom window, I witnessed the demon stuff the flapping bird into the sack. Even Dante was unprepared for the violent thrashing from within the pillowcase that followed. Not to mention the ungodly din. At first it frightened, but then delighted, him.

"Within moments I myself was in the yard uttering every incantation I could think of. But when the devil saw me, he clutched the bag and took to the rooftops. Pausing only at the peak of the stable, he hung the pitifully writhing bag from the weather vane, laughed demonically, and disappeared down the far side of the roof. Fearing what other devilment he might cause, I gave chase.

"I suspect that it was moments later when you yourselves were awakened and looked out of your windows, just as you are doing now. Unfortunately, the demon eluded me for some time, and I was unable to return here.

"When I did, however"—Mephisto's voice took on a note of sadness—"I did not act honorably—fearing I would lose my accommodations if my secret were to get out. I was, in my own way, no better than the demon, slinking back to my room. I hid in the shadows and let an innocent boy take the blame. But guilt would not let me rest." He looked directly at Eddie. "And I hope you will accept my apology." Eddie smiled and nodded.

"Now, if I may in some small way attempt to make restitution to the other parties involved." Mephisto smiled broadly and pulled a covered dish from under his cape.

"Cairo," he called to the cat. "This is for you." With a flourish he uncovered the dish and revealed a beautifully roasted fish.

The cat poked his head from his favorite bush and mewed, but Mephisto could entice him no closer.

"I can certainly understand your caution," he said, and laughed. He placed the uncovered plate a few yards from the watchful cat. "This will be here when you want it."

"And now, Judge Washington," Mephisto strode toward the judge's house and bowed slightly. "Unfortunately, I cannot undo what has been done, nor can I turn back the hands of time and restore your once proud bird to his former self. I can, however, suggest a new beginning." Reaching out, he seemed to produce a hen's egg from the chilly predawn air.

As chuckles and soft laughter rose from those watching, Mephisto pulled from his pocket a white cloth bag. He carefully placed the egg inside and then pulled the drawstring.

"And now . . ." Suddenly the suitcase began to thump and bang again, and the growls this time seemed louder.

"Dante." Mephisto
turned toward the valise.
"What did I tell you?" The
thumping became more violent, and
Mephisto started to walk toward it.
Suddenly the noise stopped. Mephisto
paused, and waited. When convinced that
the interruption was over, he smiled and raised his
hand as if to begin again.

"As I—" *BOOM!* The lid of the suitcase flew open, and an onlooker screamed. Frozen for a moment in the lantern light was a hairy, horned devil. Then the creature rose from the open trunk, casting a hellish shadow onto the fence behind. In another moment it bounded out across the yard, snatched the bag from Mephisto's outstretched hand, and leapt into the nearest tree, where it disappeared among the branches.

The magician barely had time to utter, "DANTE, STOP!" Before the demon dove from the tree to the edge of the barn roof. Bag in hand, he raced to the peak of the roof and climbed atop the weather vane. Holding the bag victoriously over his head, the demon laughed a hideous laugh, then hung the sack on one of the outstretched iron bars and vanished down the other side of the barn.

"Not again!" Mephisto cried. Grabbing his suitcase, he headed off in hot pursuit. "I'm so sorry, but I must go!" And he, too, disappeared.

The stunned silence was broken by Mrs. Murphy's commanding voice. "GO AFTER HIM, ISAIAH!" Eddie recognized the boy he had spoken to in the backyard the day before, as the boy burst from the kitchen, flew down the porch steps, and tore off after Mephisto.

A confused murmur was becoming audible when "HE'S GONE!" rang out. Isaiah was returning to the yard. "He's just gone, I tell ya!"

Then, almost with his next breath, he cried, "LOOK!" All eyes followed his pointing finger to the barn roof, where the cloth bag hung. Silhouetted against the dawn-brightened sky, IT MOVED!

Instantly the judge was barking orders, and within minutes his servants had gotten the ladder. Just like the day before, one servant waited at its base while the other two made the climb. After straddling the roof's peak to the weather vane, the first man reached out for the bag. When it jerked violently, he pulled back.

"Just grab it and bring it down here!" shouted the judge.

Holding the writhing bag at arm's length, the first servant gladly handed the bag off to the man who had waited at the top of the ladder. He, in turn, breathed a loud sigh of relief when the man on the ground hesitatingly accepted the burden.

Anticipation ran high in the small crowd of neighbors that had gathered around the impatient judge, who waited near the henhouse.

"Well, open it!" he snapped as the last servant laid the dreadful bundle at the judge's feet. The servant hesitated.

"Oh, all right," the judge barked, trying not to show any fear. "I'll do it!" He had barely loosened the drawstring when a squawking, flapping mass shot out. Everyone, including the judge, jumped back.

"Well, I never!" he exclaimed in disbelief, as a beautiful rooster fluttered to the ground.

The handsome bird stood for a moment, ruffled his feathers into place, and took another short flight to the top of the nearest fence post. Tilting his head this way and that, he surveyed the poultry yard in typical rooster fashion. Then, fluffing himself up and flapping his wings, he broke the early dawn silence with a sun-raising "Cock-a-doodle-doo!"

The neighbors cheered, and even the judge seemed delighted. Slowly the little knot of people dressed in robes and nightshirts returned to their houses. Eddie alone had stayed inside, and he now sank back onto his bed as a dazed sense of relief and pride washed over him.

"He did it!" Eddie sighed. "He actually saved my hide . . . and improved the act!"

CHAPTER FOURTEEN

The sun was several hours higher in the sky when Eddie heard a soft knock at his bedroom door.

"Master Eddie, it's breakfast time." Dap's deep voice spoke from the other side.

"Thanks, Dap. I'll be right with you." Unable to sleep, Eddie had been dressed for at least an hour, and was at the door ready to go down much more promptly than usual. Dap beamed from the hallway.

"I knew you didn't do it, Master Eddie, but I never thought the devil was the real culprit." They looked at each other, and then burst into relieved laughter.

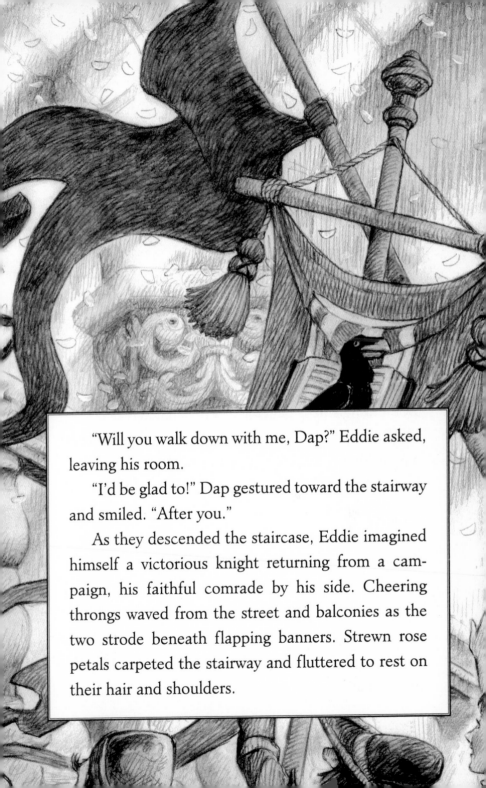

"Will you walk down with me, Dap?" Eddie asked, leaving his room.

"I'd be glad to!" Dap gestured toward the stairway and smiled. "After you."

As they descended the staircase, Eddie imagined himself a victorious knight returning from a campaign, his faithful comrade by his side. Cheering throngs waved from the street and balconies as the two strode beneath flapping banners. Strewn rose petals carpeted the stairway and fluttered to rest on their hair and shoulders.

Halfway down, Eddie breathed deeply. "Something smells delicious!" He exhaled.

"Pancakes," Dap said. "Miss Fannie knows they are your favorite, and ordered them special, so I expect you'll be enjoying your breakfast." He grew serious as they reached the dining room door. "But I'm not sure about Master Allan, though." Eddie looked up at him, puzzled. "He'll be eating crow."

Eddie clapped a hand over his mouth in an effort to stifle the eruption of laughter. Shoulders heaving, Dap turned away and walked quickly to the safety of the kitchen.

Taking a deep breath, Eddie composed himself, ran his hand over his hair, straightened his shoulders, and entered.

"This ought to be fun!" McCobber whispered.

"Eddie!" Fannie jumped up from her place at the table and ran to give him a hug. "We're so sorry, Eddie. I knew you could never have done such a thing!" She hugged him again, and they took their seats.

"Well, Edgar," said John Allan, who had barely looked up from the newspaper he was reading, "it appears that you were spared a whipping, and by the devil's own hand, at that." He turned the page. "It seems appropriate somehow, doesn't it?"

"Well, you know what they say." Eddie speared a stack of pancakes with a fork and put them on his plate. "The devil is in the details."

Fannie laughed, and then checked herself as Allan cleared his throat and looked up from his paper. "I'm not sure you are applying that adage correctly in this case."

"You might be right, sir." Eddie watched with glowing delight as the maple syrup he poured from the warmed pitcher spilled over the pancakes and dripped down the sides of the stack. "Perhaps Shakespeare said it more eloquently."

"And how's that?" Allan asked, lowering the paper.

"'There are more things in heaven and earth than are dreamt of in your philosophy'." Eddie took a bite and closed his eyes, enjoying the texture of the cakes, the taste of melted butter, the flavor of the syrup, and the extreme pleasure of the moment.

"Sweet," McCobber purred. "Very sweet!"

Epilogue

Several weeks later, Eddie received a large envelope in the mail containing a theatrical poster and a short note:

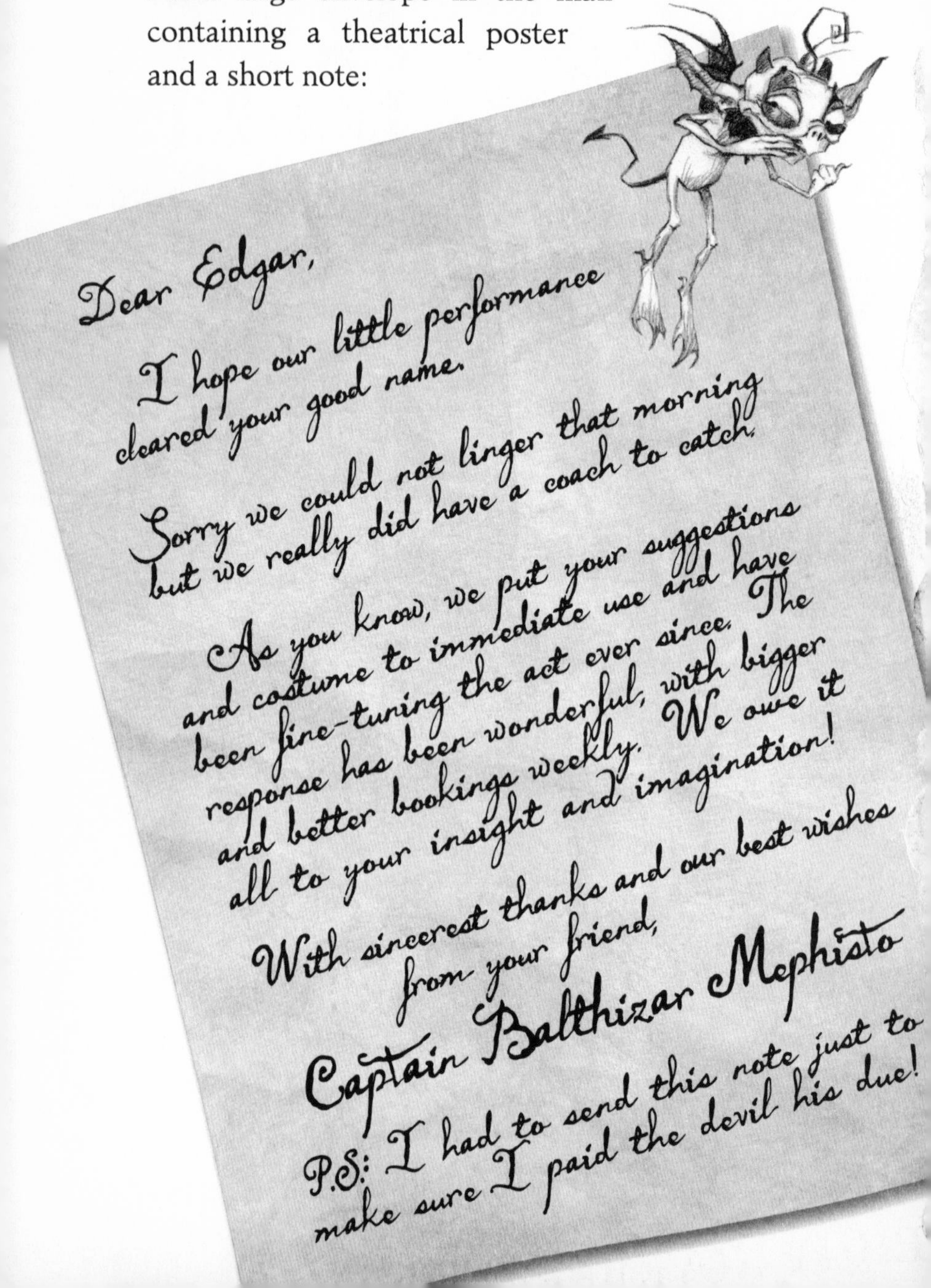

Dear Edgar,

I hope our little performance cleared your good name.

Sorry we could not linger that morning but we really did have a coach to catch.

As you know, we put your suggestions and costume to immediate use and have been fine-tuning the act ever since. The response has been wonderful, with bigger and better bookings weekly. We owe it all to your insight and imagination!

With sincerest thanks and our best wishes
from your friend,

Captain Balthizar Mephisto

P.S: I had to send this note just to make sure I paid the devil his due!

Witness
THE AMAZING
MEPHISTO

AS HE STRUGGLES TO TAME
THE **FIEND** WITHIN
The ENCHANTED CLOTH!!

Extended by Popular Demand!!
RIDAY, NOVEMBER 5ᵀᴴ

ACKNOWLEDGMENTS

There are a number of people who deserve recognition for their contributions behind the scenes.

First of all, I would like to thank my friend and colleague, Tony DiTerlizzi, whose generosity and pivotal assistance helped turn a manuscript into a book. I would also like to thank Kevin Lewis, for his initial interest and infectious enthusiasm.

At Simon & Schuster, I'd like to thank Courtney Bongiolatti for her editorial guidance, insight, and patience; Laurent Linn, whose great design sense, fine judgment, and helpful encouragement were all greatly appreciated; and Annie Zourzoukis for her copy editing expertise.

I also had the help of some very patient and willing models: Tom Gianni, Karl and Patty Gustafson, and especially Morgan Wallace, who good-naturedly endured many a tiresome photo shoot.

I am also indebted to nature photographer, Paul Lantz (paullantz.com), who generously allowed me the use of several of his stunning raven photographs as visual reference.

Thanks to Jeff London and Gerta Sorensen-London for their technical advice.

While doing research in Richmond, Virginia, I was assisted by Dana Angell Puga and Audrey C. Johnson at the Library of Virginia, and Megan Zeoli and Keith Kaufelt at the Poe Museum.

I would also like to thank my good friends, Gary Gianni and Randy Broecker, whose enthusiastic support helped keep this project afloat when it was little more than a fleeting idea.

And last, but definitely not least, my love and appreciation go to my wife, Patty, who from the first mention of a half-baked concept to the last pencil stroke on the final drawing, was there with constant encouragement. Her conscientious scanning of the artwork, artistic expertise, and technical support made this book possible. I could not have done it without her.